GRANDPA ROCKS!

By
Robert Huston

Illustrations and cover art by David Knox
Layout and Design by The Author's Press
First Printing: May 2006
Library of Congress Catalog Card: Pending
US ISBN 10: 1-933505-15-X
US ISBN 13: 978-1-933505-15-2

www.theauthorspress.com
www.grandparocks.com

GRANDPA

ROCKS!

By
Robert Huston

The Author's Press
Atlanta   Olympia   Los Angeles

FOREWARD

As you get older, one wonders what life is all about, there has to be more.

I have been one of those lucky ones that a window was opened to let me see the protective love and persuasion that exist all around us and intertwines in our lives.

We, many times, are not looking or are unaware that anything so magnificent even exists. It is only after you're in your twilight years, after many hardships and blessings that were unexplainable, then we realize we were never alone.

Part of this book I'll be sharing those years I wasn't looking for the One behind all those protective times.

As you read you'll soon see a sharing of a spiritual force that changed my life even when I wasn't looking for that form—the very beginning, when three kids stood at a cistern on the farm to the many times the Devil tried to take me out, but the God behind all of this had larger plans and so He may be glorified.

Storytelling is as old as man himself, one of the blessings God gave me was teaching His word and telling stories to whoever would listen–mainly my grandchildren.

Some of these stories are true, some made up, some a ribbon of truth running through them. You'll have to read them many times to see where the truth really is.

Good Luck.

DEDICATION

To my wife Jeannie, who puts up with me,
and for all the help.
To all of my children and their husbands.
To all of my grandchildren, who think their granddad is
a little strange.

TABLE OF CONTENTS

INTRODUCTION

I will be telling my life's story. They are the stories that the Holy Spirit has showed me over the years, and some are the experiences that we have had.

Jean and I live in Conyers, Georgia, and have for twenty-two years. I have started putting these stories together and God has guided me to the completion of this book.

One day I was at a Mennonite church where my son-in-law goes, and there was a man resting out in the shade, I just sat down and started talking to him. I started to talk to him about camping. The things we had done with our children growing up, and how our children loved to go camping, and it's probably the best thing we ever did. We talked about an old pop-up camper and tent and the times it rained on us. We spoke of how I sold the camper when the arthritis started kicking in, and then of our dream of a travel trailer for a ministry we were thinking about. He listened to me for a while and he said, "Well, my neighbor is a tech graduate and he has cancer in his lymph nodes. The cancer has gone all through his body, but right now it is in remission. I visit him quite often, and he has been telling me about the work he has done on this camper he has out in his backyard: twenty-one feet long, a set of tires, a muffler system, rebuilt motor and some added amenities inside. He and his wife, while he's still healthy, would like to go down to Florida or out west, but since he's been sick, he doesn't know whether he can do that and he may come to the position before too long where he may have to sell it. But he would like to make just one more trip before he gets too sick."

"Next time you see him, ask him what he would take for that camper."

I don't know whether I'm really interested in that, but I said see what he would take. Before I saw this man again, the gentleman who had the cancer had another attack, and he had to go to the hospital. He told our friends that he was going to have to sell the camper.

"It's no use keeping it," he said, "I'm not getting any better, and I'm not going to get better."

My friend called me up and he said, "Why don't you come down and look at it?"

I went down and I looked at the camper. It was a 1984 Travelcraft, twenty-one feet long and at the time when it was new, it was a deluxe camper. Inside, it was very, very nice.

I told the man, "Well, I'm interested in your camper. If you sell it to me, it's going to be a ministry. I'm not just buying it to sell it. I'm going to use it."

"Well, let me think about it for a while," he said.

Over the next two weeks, he got to feeling so much better that he took the camper for a ride to southern

Georgia and back, staying overnight. When he got back a week later, the cancer hit him again. So he called, "If you want the camper, Mr. Huston, you come on over, and I'll give you a price."

I felt so sorry for the man because he knew he was dying. He was a Christian and he offered me the camper and a real, real good price, and I said all right. We prayed about it, and we prayed that God would heal him. If He would heal him that I would bring that camper right back. So that's the way we left it, and a week later we went over and we got the camper and brought it home. Since that time, he has been back to the hospital, and he has passed on into the Lord's Care.

As you listen to these stories remember that God knew. God knew a year, two years or three years ahead of me knowing. He knew that I was going to put these stories together so that I could share them with others and with my grandchildren and my family. I'll probably be speaking to different clubs, different organizations and I'd have the means now to travel and to actually do it. He did it even when I wasn't ready or even thinking about doing it.

So, here we are putting all of these stories together where Christ will be glorified, and God has given me the ability to speak to groups and to share Christ. We have a camper, and now it's just a matter of putting it all together. We have a girl who is going to make the brochure for me, which will have all my stories on it. They've taken some pictures of me all dressed up and God sent me the artist for the illustrations.

God is putting this all together. He was putting this together even before we were ready. I thank God for it. I don't know where it's going to go, what's going to happen.

There is a new ministry starting. It's called 'Grandpa Rocks'. I'm going to use the prop of a rocking chair and I'm going to be dressed up; do some pantomime, sermonettes with some illustration. There are a lot of projects. Now, why has He waited until I hit seventy-nine years old? Why didn't He do it when I was fifty?

I think the reason was, spiritually, I wasn't ready. I am ready now. God is still making me creative, He's still letting me use illustrations. So, let's just thank Him.

> Praise You, Lord, praise You, Lord. Thank You for listening.

I know sometimes you wonder, "Lord, what are You doing?" Well, whatever He is doing, it has to be right.

JOAN AND AL

There was a young couple that Jean and I met as young Christians. My wife and I had a hard year the year before we went to camp and discovered married life to be more than we had bargained for. We realized that our marriage vows, "to death do us part," had nothing to do with kids. More kids and bills had more to do with lack of quality time, burn-out and overworked–that seems to run together. The balance that makes a good marriage seems to get lost. Well, every couple experiences this, and I know that we did.

In this aftermath of fear, Jean and I came to the conclusion that we needed a vacation, just anywhere away from the mundane way of life. Now, we know God was in it but, Lord, we didn't know it was going to be this hard. So newspaper clippings and brochures began to pile up, and a lot of help from friends who know just the spot where we could go to unwind with our three kids. But we soon learned that vacations that took children cost a lot of money. And we were far away from that, which meant that more money had to come to get us to where we were going.

We started to pray, "Lord, we need some quality time together, and we need some money, if You're still there, and if we're gonna be able to even begin to get this vacation."

We finally after prayer, chose a Christian camp on the eastern edge of the Pennsylvania. It was started by the late Percy Crawford, who at that time was recovering from a very severe heart attack. Now we had a place to go, but money was the question. Now I deduced that if we don't eat and buy things we don't need, and if I can coast in my car whenever I could to save gas, and if I drove thirty miles per hour instead of fifty and sixty, we could save enough. And if we used as little food as possible—well, we were desperate. After all, we wanted to go.

The time to send in our application finally arrived. With much anticipation, we sent them in and we almost didn't do it. But what God had planned for us was one of the greatest blessings in our lives. The day came when we started packing our Ford station wagon. I'm sure glad it had a large back compartment, because clothes for three kids with their favorite pillows and toys, and food to keep them quiet while we road, plus Jean's and my clothes completely filled it up. The kids hardly slept that first night before we left. I couldn't believe we really were going to have some time together. And, it would be paid for.

Thank You, Lord!

This is something about turning out of your driveway and heading east with the excitement of the unknown that becomes very refreshing. After hours of driving, we finally arrived at Percy Crawford's camp. It was more than we had ever dreamed. The kids saw the playground and the swimming pool and, yes, other kids their own age.

What a place for a vacation! We checked in and found everything to be so clean and so neat, and along with the kids, what a place for a vacation! Lord, I guess You know what You are doing. Amen.

We met a young couple next door to us that was from New York. We seemed to be having a lot in common, if first impressions mean anything. We became friends and glad that we were next door. It just so happened that in the dining hall, a section was set apart for parents with their children, but the Lord started to implant His plan, and sent the people from New York at our table. It was a great, big round table. It was big and round enough for everybody and still had room, so we all could see each other and talk and share good food in an easy atmosphere.

This table over the week's time became a table of real fellowship—of close friendship, trusting one another, a place to ask questions about things of the Lord. God was working in these young Christians and our lives, and we weren't aware of it yet. So, let's go back to a year before this special vacation.

George Soltaun, pastor of the Presbyterian Church had preached a series of sermons on knowing God and how He relates in our lives. Well, I have to tell you a truth. I don't remember any of these sermons, but God had implanted in Jean's and my mind most of the things George had said.

You see, all that week, Joan and Al, coming from a Catholic background were full of questions. They were as close to a spiritual sponge that you'll ever find. They would ask us questions on any subject, George had preached a sermon on one year before, and we both knew the answer and how to apply it. Wow, that blows my mind, even as I relate this story now.

Now, it is best for women to talk to women and men to men in these kinds of situations, but we grew so comfortable with each other that it just didn't matter. Sometimes Joan and I kept kids, and Jean and Al went to the meetings at night. And sometimes it was the other way around.

By the end of the week, Joan and Al were very close to asking God to come into their lives and be in their hearts. What I'm about to tell you now is one of those things that only God could have worked out.

It was the last meeting, last day, big spiritual high. Joan was putting her kids to sleep and having a hard time getting them down. I didn't wait on her, and I went on ahead and set about halfway down in the auditorium.

The music was heavenly. The speakers were inspired. Now, the Decision time came before we all went home. I started to thank God for bringing Jean and I to the camp and providing the money, when suddenly Joan and Al came upon my heart. It was a tremendous burden. The invitation was given and I didn't know if Joan and Al was even there.

Had they made it? I don't know, but I prayed anyway. Then the second invitation came, and the burden came upon my heart heavier and heavier than I have ever known. Now, the third and last invitation was given, and I prayed God, "If Joan and Al are here, Lord, take my life if need be, but don't let them leave this place until you save their souls."

All of a sudden a peace came over me like I've never known. Jean was praying back in the cabin, and I knew that I knew, that I knew that something tremendous had happened. Praise God!

Well, the place was packed and I was halfway down the aisle, and a lot of people came to know Christ that evening. Between hugs and congratulations, it took me twenty minutes to get out the door. I no more took ten steps, and Joan was tapping on my arm.

She said, "Bob, Bob, guess what? I've accepted Christ as my Savior?" I'm glad that it was dark, because tears were coming down my face. And then she said, "It was on the third time they asked for people to accept Christ. I just couldn't resist anymore."

I knew that I knew that I knew. Wow. And I knew when she accepted Christ, even though I didn't know that she was behind me. We walked arm in arm away from the crowd, and she started to talk about her life, coming to know Al, falling in love, to living in a Catholic neighborhood, and their kids had to kiss Mary's feet. She was bothered by that very much. She didn't want her kids to do that, but she didn't know why. She said that she knew that all of this was wrong, but didn't know until now that she met Jean and I, and then she started to cry. All those years in her life, and in her new relived life in Christ came out. I held her, and let it all come out.

By now the meeting had been over for an hour. It was very dark, but time stood still. A new Christian came into the world. We walked back to our cabin and under the lights of the street lamp it finally dawned on me, we were an hour late with another man's wife, and she had been crying. And Al was bigger than me. Jean knows how to add two and two.

"Oh Lord, oh Lord," I said.

We walked Joan to her door. She knocked and Al opened the door with a jerk, took one look at her and one look at me. Thank God, Joan said this: "Honey, I just accepted Christ as my personal Savior." He took another look at me again, pulled her into the room, and slammed the door.

Jean was very quiet, but a good listener. We both praised God. Now the next morning, I just knew Al was going to kill me, but God intervened. We left the cabin together to go to breakfast, and Al came up to me, shook my hand, and thanked me and Jean for being part of their life and being understanding of Joan.

I said, "Well, our hope is you will come to know the Lord before you leave here." Well, I just didn't know what else to say.

He said, "I want to, but my job, my relatives, and where I live is going to make it very hard. But, I could do it secretly."

We parted that day as Christian friends and a day doesn't go by that I don't wonder how God has worked all that out. Someday, I will know, but you know, the Devil must have been very, very furious., which is the rest of the story.

We left the camp about 10:30 that morning and headed west across Pennsylvania. It was a most beautiful, beautiful day. We were on a spiritual high, and I know that whoever is reading this story has experienced this many, many times. The kids fell asleep, and we listened to good music. Now, I was in no hurry to get home, and I didn't want to go fast down the road because loaded, my car was so heavy. So I was going about fifty-five miles an hour.

What a day! I still remember it. Cars were passing us like we were standing still. All of a sudden, we had a flat tire; the right back tire blew out. Now, I had good tires on my car. I'm ashamed to tell this, but I forgot all about God as I was unpacking the back, and God became very, very far away from my mind. I finally got the tire out and was ready to change it. I had just got it out, the State Patrol had pulled up. He asked me where we came from and where we were going. When he found out we had been to Percy Crawford's camp, he was elated, because he and his family had been there the year before. Leave it to the Lord to lead me back to His Spiritual Roots with a Christian State Patrolman. We looked at the flat tire and it was perfectly good, but the sidewall had blown out. About that time, an emergency call came on the policeman's radio. He took off, tires smoking, and the kids just loved it. We got everything back in the car and started west once more. We drove about forty-five minutes, and up ahead we saw the patrol car's lights blinking and about six to eight cars piled up on one terrible wreck, with dead people lying on the road.

Our new Christian patrolman waved us on. About half an hour down the road we started to put what we had just seen together. The Devil was furious. Let me explain.

We were driving fifty-five miles per hour, almost a mile a minute. From where we had that flat to the wreck, would have put the Christian family right in the middle of it. In the time it took to change the tire, we would have been there, too.

I wrote down eight things that happened that day. God had taken Jean and I across the state of Pennsylvania and had paid for our vacation when we prayed. He helped us choose a Christian camp. He put Joan and Al next door and at the same table. There was a need there, you know the story. George Soltaun's sermon had prepared us one year in advance and we have been very humbled.

Now, that just doesn't happen. He kept Al from killing me. Now, that has to be from the Lord. He put a hole in a perfectly good tire. He brought Al's family to the Lord and they went back into a Catholic neighborhood that doesn't know the Lord. We had one of the most enjoyable vacations in our Christian growth. Now that's the rest of the story, and I think you can understand and see that only God could have brought this about. Only God could do it. If we hadn't prayed, we would have never gone. If we hadn't prayed, we would have probably been in the hospital, all of us, and maybe dead. He had something more for Jean and I to do, and our family in the years to come. We only had three children then, now we have five. Each one of these girls have married Christian men, and they're raising Christian families. So, you see God is in control, and I have very humbled by even telling this story.

Now, I'm now sure what I'm going to give you next, but maybe I'll give you my life's story to tie this all together, then give you the stories that God has given me over the years.

Thank you for listening.

WHAT A MESS!

The Day The Team Ran Off
Ten years old, 1937, My home on the Kelso farm

My father was manager of the farm and orchard
owned by Mr. Kelso. At that time we had two teams of
horses on the farm. One of the mares had a colt that we
kids tried to make into our pet. We watched the miracle
of the colt's birth, and stared in awe as it stood up almost
immediately. It knew instinctively where to go to find its
milk. Its mom surely didn't tell it. We saw firsthand how
God created animals, and how they just knew what to do.

The colt got used to us, but we couldn't train it; it had
a mind of its own. Over time, he grew up to be a young
horse who had done nothing but run around in the field
and eat. The time had come when he was needed to do
some work on the farm. He didn't understand work, but
he did know what play and freedom was all about.

We had a rather large wagon, Mr. Kelso and my dad
thought they would hook him up to the wagon alongside
his mother. At least she would be familiar to him! They

put him in his own barn stall and let him get used to my dad. Dad would brush him down and talk to him daily. After a couple of weeks, Dad would walk into the stall and put a blanket over his back. At first the colt wasn't sure if he liked that. Then one day, Dad had a harness with him and he laid it on the young horse's back. Everything went well.

Later that weekend, Dad put the horse collar on him. Then the harness again and tightened it up. The colt went crazy, bucking, kicking and throwing himself around the stall. Dad got out of the stall immediately until the colt calmed down. Then Dad took this all off the colt. This process continued everyday, for a couple of weeks.

After all this, he put the bridle on the colt's head. It was the first time the colt had a hard bit in his mouth. Things went so well, that they led the colt around outside in the barnyard. Tomorrow was going to be the colt's first day to be in the harness with his mother alongside, hitched to the wagon.

My mother, Mrs. Kelso, and us kids were standing up by the corn crib well out of the way. The mare was hooked up. Mr. Kelso led the colt alongside his mother, and Dad hooked him up. He was just prancing around, he thought it was playtime. All went well. Dad took the lines and crawled into the wagon, and then he gave the order, "Get up."

The mare moved ahead and the wagon bumped the colt's backside. He didn't know what had happened. Dad said, "Whoa" and pulled the lines tighter. The colt began to feel the bit in his mouth tighten and began to relax with the command.

"Get up, whoa."

"Get up, whoa."

So far, so good. They went to the right and then to the left in large circles. In fact, all was going so well, that Dad decided to take the team down the road. He had turned around and was coming back toward the barn when something happened.

Two tom cats came out of the weeds, chasing a female cat. They came out clawing, scratching, and pitching a fight right in front of the colt. The suddenness of it unnerved the colt and the mare, and they took off running down the road at a full gallop. Dad put his foot up on the front of the wagon and pulled on the lines as hard as he could.

"Whoa, whoa, whoa." He set the brake and the two back wheels were sliding. "Whoa, whoa."

The dust was flying. Dad and the runaway team were coming down the road toward the barn. Mr. Kelso was standing in the middle of the road waving his arms and his hat. Mrs. Kelso, my mom and us kids were up by the corn crib out of the way. Some were crying, and I wet my pants! We were all yelling, "Whoa, whoa."

We were all afraid for my dad because the horses were not paying any attention to his commands! We had a full blown runaway team! They almost ran over Mr. Kelso. I can still see Dad's face was as white as a sheet. As the runaways made that right turn in front of them, there was a large electric pole. The colt went to the right, and the mare went to the left. They came together on the other side of the pole. The colt fell down, the wagon tongue broke and both horses were shaking all over.

Dad went flying out of the wagon, rolling down the hill and skinning up both arms to the point of bleeding!

Mr. Kelso picked himself up off the road. My dad and he both ran and grabbed one of the horses by their halters and tried to calm them down. Up on the hill, we were still by the corn crib, afraid to move. What a mess those two tom-cats caused!

Mr. Kelso and Dad finally got the horses untangled and put back in their stall. No one was seriously hurt. Mr. Kelso said he didn't think that the mare would work along with the colt anymore because of his skittish ways. Dad agreed.

The next week, a neighbor called Charles, came and got that colt. He was going to train him to work and take instructions. All I can say is when the colt came back to the farm, he was one of the best horses we ever had.

KNUCKLEHEAD

I was eight years old, and staying on my Grandpa's farm, located outside of Enon Valley. I helped with different chores, like feeding the chickens, pigs, horses and cows. I gave them hay and grain. I learned how to milk a cow.

Now, Grandpa had a set of mules on his farm and one of the mules, the male mule, was called Knucklehead. On Monday morning after breakfast, we would go to the corn crib and sack corn, and then go to the granary and sack up oats and wheat, and then place all the sacks in a buckboard wagon. We could load up twenty or thirty sacks in Grandpa's buckboard.

Grandpa was going to take it to the feed mill in Enon Valley. I had been on Grandpa's farm several different times, but I had never had a chance to go to the feed mill early in the morning with him before. When I asked why we went to the feed mill, he told me that the feed mill, is where the corn, oats and wheat were ground up for cow feed. I knew that I was going to get a chance to drive Grandpa's team.

It was an honor, a real honor to drive Grandpa's team. We hooked up Knucklehead and Bess, Grandpa's other mule, to the buckboard and we waved goodbye to Grandma, and we headed for the mill. About a mile down the road, Grandpa says, "You want to drive, Bob?"

"I sure do, " I replied. I drove that team down through the country, and at least three or four miles to the feed mill. Now, this feed mill was owned by Jean's granddad. While the corn and the wheat were being ground, all the farmers gathered around and got caught up on all the news that was happening in the country. They talked about the prices of pigs, what cows were going for, who had died and who was sick, and who wasn't at church last Sunday. It seemed to me that Grandpa just wasn't in a hurry at all.

We needed to make one stop before we started home and that was at the country store to get some things that Grandma wanted. Now, one of the things that I liked was corn flakes. In those days, the boxes were huge, I mean they were really big boxes of corn flakes. Grandma would give Grandpa a big list, and I got my corn flakes and whatever else that she had ordered. When we came out of the store, another farmer had pulled up alongside our buckboard wagon, and Knucklehead was making his ears just go back and forth, back and forth, and he was making a funny noise and prancing. I never had seen him do that before.

"Grandpa, do you know what's wrong with Knucklehead?"

He just smiled at me and said, "That horse right there, it's a she."

"What?"

Grandpa Rocks!

"It's a girl horse."

Well, I didn't know anything about that, why Knucklehead would be so excited just because he was standing beside a girl horse. I never knew when Grandpa was serious or not, so I just figured he was joking, and let that one go.

Well, we left for home from the country store early in the afternoon, and we didn't get home until it was really late in the afternoon. Now, Grandma was scolding Grandpa for taking all that time and talking so much, but it seemed to me, that she wanted to know everything that was going on. Well, Grandpa would listen as she would scold him, and then he would just go on about his business. They did this all the time.

At the end of the evening, when all the chores were done, we would sit on the front porch. First, Grandpa would sit down and listen to the evening news. He decided when the radio was on, when the radio was off, and what we would listen to. So sitting on the porch, listening to the radio with Grandma on the swing and Grandpa in his rocking chair with a corncob pipe with smoke all around his head, was a nice summer evening at Grandpa's farm. I would just sit there and watch the bugs make a left or a right, or turn and make a loop to get out of Grandpa's smoke until it was dark and I couldn't see anymore. No mosquitoes or bugs of any kind flew into Grandpa's smoke.

Grandma was dying to hear of all the news Grandpa had heard at the feed mill and at the country store, she wanted to know every detail. Now, they had a game that they played. She would ask, he would tell, slowly, very slowly. It took hours for Grandpa to tell Grandma everything he heard.

All of a sudden, a big bang was coming from the barn, and then it was all quiet. Then another big bang came from the barn again.

"Grandpa, what was that?" I asked.

"Knucklehead, that dumb mule is having a dream. He's kicking the side of the stall," and then Grandpa laughed. "He's probably thinking about that girl horse at the store."

At this time the electric company was putting in poles to run wires to bring the first electric lights into Grandpa's house. The electric company had dug a large pit in the corner of Grandpa's barnyard. It was for the stumps, pieces of the light log, and other trash from the construction. When they were done, they would fill the rest of the hole in with dirt, but they hadn't used that pit–yet.

One night, Knucklehead was dreaming and not only kicked his stall but he had bit through the rope that was tying him to the stall and got loose. Now, you can imagine a dumb mule getting out into the barnyard, sleep walking?

Knucklehead didn't know anything about that pit, and he fell head first right into that hole. Grandpa got up about 5:00 a.m. and saw the barn door open and he knew that mule was out, but there were chores to be done and that came first over looking for the mule. Chores were done, and Grandma was cooking breakfast, when Grandpa came into the kitchen to eat.

"Grandma, you know what that dumb mule did last night?"

Grandpa Rocks!

"What now?"

"Well, he bit through his rope and he kicked open the barn door, and Lord knows where he's at and the gate is open too."

"Oh, maybe he fell into that pit, Grandpa."

"He's not that dumb. Pass the eggs, please."

After breakfast, Grandpa started for the barn walking right past the pit when he heard a chopping noise coming from the pit. He looked into that hole, and what he saw made him mad, but also made him laugh so hard he was bent over. There were tears coming down his cheeks, when Grandpa starting talking in what Grandma calls 'heavenly language'.

Grandpa went to the feed mill and to the country store, and told everyone that the electric company had dug a huge hole in the corner of the barnyard. If anybody had any garbage they wanted to get rid of it, bring it and dump it into that hole in the barnyard.

At first nothing happened, and then Mr. Scott who lived on the next farm had a fourteen acre field of pumpkins he had raised that year, not all of them were sold. The rest were garbage and could be brought over. So he asked Sam if he could bring his garbage, and Sam said, "Yep."

Well, Mr. Scott backed his truck up to that hole, unhooked the tailgate, and that's when he saw that mule. He said, "Sam, what in the. . . ? What are you doing? There's a mule down in that hole."

Grandpa said, "Yep."

"Do you really want me to dump those pumpkins there?"

"Yep."

So, Mr. Scott raised the bed of that truck and dumped all of those rotten pumpkins down on that mule's head. They rained over his shoulders and down his back. What a mess!

Mr. Scott had no sooner got home than he telephoned all his neighbors about the mule in the pit, and everything Grandpa was doing. The whole county was laughing, and everybody started to bring in their garbage.

Now, you gotta understand, we all have a telephone and in those days, everybody picked it up, and everybody listened in. It was one of those lines where everybody could listen anytime, called a party line. So, Mr. Scott had to make only one telephone call.

Poor old Knucklehead.

They poured garbage over his head and down over his back, and all over his feet. That old mule started moving his ears back and forth, back and forth. He was thinking, and he started to stamp that garbage under his feet, and he started to raise one inch at a time. Everyday he raised one more inch. Then one day, three weeks later, old Knucklehead rose to the top.

There's a moral to my story and it is this: Garbage that comes into your life, no matter how little or how big, can be shaken off and used to climb to the top. Just lift your head. Shake your shoulders and let it roll off. Stamp your feet and let it roll right under your feet, and you will rise one inch higher. You need to rise above your circumstances, and go on with life. Wiggle your ears and start thinking. God's got something better for you, so turn it over to Him.

APPLE GREEN OUTHOUSE

On Halloween every once in a while, someone would have their outhouse pushed over. I should tell you that there are three types of outhouses, depending on the seating arrangement. There are one holers, two holers, and three holers! Most had an old Sears catalog sitting within arm's reach. Sometimes they had a placard on the door, which read "Meditation Room!"

The county store owner had made a statement, "No one is going to push his outhouse over." He slipped out late at night on Halloween and sat in his outhouse, just waiting to catch some young men in the act.

Five of these young men came up to the backside of his outhouse and pushed it over with the door down on the ground. So Mr. Lusk was trapped inside his own outhouse. He had not told his wife what he was going to do, so he spent all night trapped inside until she found him the next morning. The fellows at the feed mill came over and set it back up, freeing Mr. Lusk! I am telling you this true story to tell you what Mr. Lusk did the next year.

Robert Huston

He wasn't going to get upset again! Mr. Lusk built a new three holer. He stained the inside and painted the outside apple green with a black shingle roof. It was a thing of beauty. He did something to keep it from being pushed over. Around the foundation he had poured cement, and placed bolts in the foundation, bolting the outhouse to it. That should have solved the problem!

Now, on Halloween everyone that bought groceries from the store started a lottery to see if it would stand. I should tell you that most outhouses stood at the back of one's property. Mr. Lusk's did too, but it was close to the railroad tracks.

Now we don't know, to this very day, who did this, but around four a.m. someone tied a heavy rope around the outside of that outhouse and when the mail train went through very slowly, they hooked the other end of the rope to the train. In one swoop, the top of that apple green outhouse came off, and it was the only three holes that had air conditioning.

KNUCKLEHEAD'S BERRIES

Of the two mules we had on the farm, Bessie was the best to pull the corn cultivator. She would stay in the rows better. You could lay the halter straps on her neck, and she wouldn't go right or left without any struggle. To our dismay, Grandpa hooked up Knucklehead to the stone boat! Just as we started walking down the lane I knew it was going to be a bad day! As I sat on the saddle blanket, we started down the lane. Knucklehead would constantly be reaching for grass on both sides, never holding his head up, even with Grandpa walking right beside us. I almost fell off two or three times.

By the time we got to the corn field, I was just crying, mad or maybe both! Knucklehead was hooked up to the cultivator, and we started down the row. To my surprise that mule walked right down the center of that corn row with Grandpa guiding the cultivator. The rows were long, and I almost fell asleep to the rocking of the mule walking.

We had fifteen rows almost done when Knucklehead started to throw his head from side to side. Sometimes he tried to nibble my feet, scaring me. On about the seventeenth row, he started weaving right and left of the center of the row.

Grandpa yelled, "Keep him in the center of the row."

I'd pull on the reins and that hard-mouthed sucker would put his head down and pay no attention to me. My arms were getting tired, and I was mad and crying.

Grandpa yelled, "Keep him in the middle of the row."

By the end of the twentieth row, he sped up and Grandpa was getting tired and sweaty trying to control the cultivator. Grandpa didn't want to speed up and he was yelling at me, "Hold him back, hold him back."

My arms were so tired, I couldn't pull any harder. We only had five more rows of corn to cultivate and then the afternoon would be over. I was wrong, wrong, wrong!

When we got almost to the end of the twenty-first row Knucklehead made a beeline for a bunch of blackberry bushes, full of big, black, ripe blackberries at the end of the row against the fence! Grandpa grabbed hold of the cultivator while taking out stalk after stalk of corn, yelling, "Hold him back, hold him back." That mule never stopped until his head was buried deep in the blackberry bush, and he was eating the blackberries.

I jumped off, crying and mad, Grandpa laid the lines to that mule's backside. He paid us no attention at all until all the blackberries were gone. Grandpa lifted me back up on Knucklehead's back, and that mule turned around and went straight down the middle of that row at the right speed. I didn't have to touch the line once.

If you have ever owned a mule, there are some days that you admire them, and then others you would like to hit them with a two by four. This might not be politically correct in 2006, but in 1939 it was.

GRANDPA'S PIPE

Now, I had worked with Grandpa for about four years off and on, so now I am about twelve years old. I can do the milking myself, I drive the team, make hay, cultivate corn, but there's one thing I have not done at twelve years old. I'd been watching Grandpa for four years do something every night that he really enjoys. That one thing is smoking his corncob pipe. He always smoked it after dinner.

Sitting in his favorite chair, he would listen to Gabriel Heeter, the only newsman of his day, and he always started out his news program, "Oh, there's good news tonight." That was his thing he would always say, and Grandpa would be smoking his old corncob pipe.

Grandpa would get in his favorite rocking chair on the porch, repack his old corncob pipe, set there, meditate, and smoke until it was dark. After watching this routine for four years, I came to the conclusion one thing I had not done is smoke, and if I'm going to be a man, I better try it. . . the sooner the better. I didn't have a plan, so the Devil helped me out.

Next Sunday morning, I played sick and didn't have to go to church. Grandpa whispered to Grandma as they left, "I think our grandson is up to something. Let's go along with it and see what he's up to."

Now, to the very bottom of this story is very important. Because at the very bottom of the pipe is where all of the juices collect. . . where it is the strongest. You never smoke it to the very bottom.

I played sick. They left for church. And the Devil had a field day with me. Now Sam's pipe really had a strong smell, but that didn't stop my plan. I wanted to be a man. I filled it with tobacco, packed it down, but not too tight. If it was too tight, the fire would go out. I had it packed just right so the air would flow through nice and even, and I could smoke it clean to the bottom. I did it right.

I lit the corncob and started to puff and started to fill the room with smoke. I started walking around the room just like Sam. Just like he did, as he listened to the news. I knew it down pat. I'd watched him for four years. I was simply doing everything, and everything was going great. Every time I puffed, I took a deep breath, and then blew it out. I was coming along fine. But I remembered that Grandpa Sam was sitting in his rocking chair, so I set down, taking deep breaths and blowing out smoke.

Now, the corncob was getting hotter and hotter, and I was almost to the bottom where the really juicy tobacco was. And I didn't know I should set the pipe back up on the mantle then. I took deep breaths. It burned all the way down and the pipe was getting hotter and hotter. I decided that that's enough of that. I stood up and the room started going round and round and round. And I sat back down in Sam's rocker. I got up slowly. I had one thought, to get the pipe back on the mantle so they wouldn't know. I forgot all about the smoke in the room. And I started to get sick. Ooo, did I get sick. . . I mean really sick. My head was spinning. I made it to the backyard and lost all of my breakfast. Now, if you've read some of the other stories, you'd know that Grandma had good breakfasts.

About that time, I heard Grandpa's car coming down the road. What to do? What to do? Where to go? What to do? Devil, where are you? I need you, there's something about the Devil. Once he gets you in trouble, he leaves you. I was on my own.

The front door opened, and they came in. The smoke hit them in the face. Grandpa walked over to the mantle, picked up his pipe, burning his fingers so bad that he dropped it to the floor and the stem broke off. Now, they started looking for me.

"Bobby, where are you? Where are you, Bobby? BOBBY! WHERE ARE YOU?" They found me on the back porch lying on the swing, sicker than a dog, and I mean sick. When they saw me they started laughing.

Grandpa said, "I see you're still sick, Bobby. Well, we'll get a little dinner in ya, and that'll make you feel better. Grandma's making your favorite meal. We'll tell you when it's ready."

I thought to myself, "Food, don't even want to smell food! I don't even want any type of food," and fell asleep. It wasn't long until Grandpa was shaking me. I stood up and my head was still going round and round. I don't know how I made it to the table, and the smell of food was awful.

Grandpa, who's still mad about his favorite pipe being broken, put a big helping of mashed potatoes and a bigger helping of noodles with meat on my plate in the middle of the potatoes. He had given me a double portion, and then smiled at me.

Now, the potatoes didn't slide down very well, and then come to slippery noodles. All I can say is that each bite went down and up at least three times. Grandpa and Grandma just set there grinning at me. And I said, "Devil, where are you? You had a plan!"

After the last bite, I headed for the garden and lost all Grandma's meal. While I was doing that, Grandpa was hollering at me, "Come on back, Bobby. Grandma made your favorite dessert. Slippery banana pudding."

I said to myself, "Drop dead, Devil! Where are you?"

Now, here are some things I have learned. The Devil will let you get into trouble, and he will also leave you high and dry. That's his plan; when you make a bad decision, you're going to suffer, and you're going to suffer on your own, and if you ever decide to smoke, you've got to be dumber than you look.

Sam, when he smoked his pipe, he never inhaled it. He just puffed it. I didn't know that. I took a deep breath each time. Now, Sam and Lucy never scolded me or even brought up about smoking a pipe. Years later they never brought it up, I also learned that if I ever decided to smoke again, I have got to be dumber than I look.

The next Sunday, I was dressed and ready to go to church, and every Sunday after that, I was dressed and ready to go to church.

DAVID AND GOLIATH

Well, you also know that the Bible talks about a man who was named Goliath. He was a very, very big man. I have heard that he was over seven feet tall, even eight foot tall. So, I take it that Goliath was a big man, bigger than most. He was man who did not believe in the God of Heaven and that he was very rough. He would do anything he could to disgrace the Lord, and he had railed against the Lord for forty days before David came into the story.

The Israelite army was on one side, and Goliath's army was on the other side. Everyday Goliath would come out, blasting the Lord. The Israelites were to send their best warrior to fight against Goliath, but no man took up the challenge, but there was one.

This news got back to David. He was taking care of sheep out on the hillside when the news of the stalemate came to him.

David stated, "Well, it's not the challenge that I'm going to go up against Goliath, but I will not have anybody talk against my Lord that way."

So, David came to the camp and his brothers and other individuals said, "This is not a job for a boy."

"Well, I'm going to defend my Lord," said David, and so they gave David armor and a shield and a sword, and I believe it was all too heavy for him. He wasn't big enough to carry all this into battle.

Stripping himself of the armor he said, "I will take my slingshot, and I will kill this giant in the name of the Lord, the God of Israel."

David came down off the hill and into the valley. There stood this big giant ready to do battle. He laughed when he saw this young boy coming down to meet him. Then he railed at him and said everything he could in the worst way against the God of Israel. David went down to the stream and picked up five smooth stones.

Well, if you study the numbers in the Bible, you will find that the number five coincides with God's Grace. So he picks up five smooth stones. Five, that represented God's Grace. Now, Goliath didn't realize that he had railed forty days, and he didn't realize that was the time of trials and pestilence in his life. Here was the case that a young boy with God's Grace coming up against a man that was going to go through trial and pestilence, was going to see who was going to win.

The head of Goliath's spear was nine pounds. Now, just to hold that spear and to throw it, you would have to be very, very strong. He was a very, very strong man, but he had a wicked heart, and he was going through trial and pestilence that day.

Well, there stood the young boy with five smooth stones. Goliath covered from head to toe with armor, just started laughing and laughing and laughing. There was no vital spot for that stone to strike. When he was railing and laughing, he raised up his head, and right between his eyes was exposed. David knew that he had to put that stone right on its mark; so he wound up his sling shot and said, "In the name of the God of Israel, He has given you into my hands."

Just as Goliath railed back and started laughing, David let go of that stone and hit him right between the eyes. The big giant fell, hit the ground, and was out cold.

David said, "The God of Israel has been avenged." He takes the sword off Goliath, raises it and cuts off his head.

Well, God was avenged. The Grace of God won that battle. And the trials of pestilence of Goliath was over. He had lost.

GENERAL WASHINGTON

General Washington and his troops had just finished a battle against the British during the Revolutionary war. During the battle most of the horses had been killed on both sides, and a lot of the men had died on both sides, but Washington's army had won the day. Well, at least they thought they had.

As they were regrouping, they spotted another British army coming from the opposite direction from where they had defeated one British army. Washington's army had no cannon set up toward that British army, and they knew they would be overrun just in a matter of minutes. There was a big man there that was called Goliath on the Washington side. And he said, "Put the cannon on my back, and I will carry it to the east side and we will save the day."

It took eight men to set up the cannon to get it up on Goliath's back. He put a rope around his shoulders and carried that cannon over to the east side. The other men took the wheels of the cannon and set them up, and then Goliath set the cannon back down in that position on the east side.

Because of that act of bravery and strength, Washington won the day. That cannon weighed over eleven hundred pounds. Goliath carried it on his back, which was an act of strength, but you have heard many, many stories where people under situations where heroics had to be performed had supernatural strength. Well, Goliath had supernatural strength that day, and Washington won the battle.

Washington was so appreciative of what Goliath had done, that they had a special sword made just for him. It was a sword that no man could swing but Goliath. . . in Washington's army.

Washington was a praying man, he believed in God and read his Bible daily. He put his faith in the God of Grace. That's the story of Goliath in the Bible and Goliath in Washington's army.

GRANDPA DUNCAN'S VIOLIN

Grandpa Duncan, when he was twelve years old, lived in the Enon Valley area of Pennsylvania. Mr. Watt was a country fiddler, and Grandpa was interested in music and him. Watt took him under his wing.

There was a sale where a violin came up for bid. Now, it wasn't much of a violin and I don't know what they paid for it, but it wasn't a great amount of money. Mr. Watt took Grandpa aside and taught him to play the country music of that day. Now this was back over about one hundred and fifty years, actually. It was what they played in the hill country of West Virginia and Kentucky, the old barn dance type of music. Of course, they still play it today.

If you grew up with it, it is one of your favorite types of music. We grew up with it, and Jean and I would go to a hoedown. Now, on Saturday evenings, we go to Newborn Opry, which is south of where we now live. The country folks come in and sing and play the old time music. Sometimes they have the old gospel songs and singers also, or a country fair. . . a little country fair with different music. People come from all over the country. So this is back to when I was a kid, I heard this type of music and it's still in my blood, even today. In fact, last Saturday evening we went to Newborn and heard country folks just having fun.

Well, Grandpa learned to play this fiddle and he got quite good at it. When he wasn't playing the fiddle, in Enon Valley, he worked in the stockyard. The train from Pittsburgh came out to Enon Valley–about fifty miles. There was a great big turntable that they put the engine on and turned the engine around and hooked it to the other end of the train, so they could take it back to Pittsburgh. So, there was a stockyard there, and some of the meat went back to Pittsburgh. Now, the reason they didn't go any further was because there weren't any rails laid any further than Enon Valley at that time.

So Grandpa was working in the stockyard, and Mr. Watt was teaching him how to play the fiddle. Then he started to play around different spots in the country, different dances. There was a young girl named Lucy and she was probably the nicest looking girl in all the community. She had an hourglass figure, was very pretty, and was just a nice person to be around. My grandpa took a shine to this Lucy, and Lucy kind of took a shine to my grandpa, Samuel Duncan. They went to many, many dances, and in the years to come they started dating, and he took her as his girlfriend to the dances.

He must have been very tolerant because as he was the country fiddler, the main one in the band, the other boys had to dance with Lucy, so I guess that all balanced out. They had a good time, they grew up and they fell in love.

Grandpa Rocks!

Later on, Grandpa bought a farm just outside of Enon Valley, and this farm was up at the end of a hollow. There were four or five farms on this road, and he was at the very end. This is the farm that I spent my summers at and worked for Grandpa. He must have paid me a little bit, but I got my room and board all summer long. This relieved my mother and father of taking care of me in the summertime, and wondering what to do with me while they worked. I enjoyed being on Grandpa's farm.

Now, Grandpa, even in Jean's time. . . she lived in Enon Valley. . . played dances in the Odd Fellows Hall in Enon Valley. The Odd Fellows Hall was where everybody met. Downstairs was a barber shop and a little store, and upstairs was the Enon Valley Odd Fellows Hall where they had barn dances and where the Eastern Star met. That building even had a third floor, not too many places around had a third floor. So, when she was a kid, Jean remembers Grandpa Duncan playing in the Odd Fellows Hall.

They did something in the community that they don't do today. You hear the words "barn dance" and know that hay season was coming up. The farmer would sweep out the barn floor. Now there's still some hay left in from the winter, but most of that had been eaten up by the cattle during the winter. They would sweep out the barn floor, it wasn't particularly level and everything, but it was cleaned out. Then all the neighbors would be invited and in the evening they would come over. The people that could play instruments would come. Us kids would get up in the hayloft and watch all of our neighbors barn dance on the barn floor. This is why they called it a barn dance.

We would have one on a Saturday night at Grandpa's farm, then next Saturday night we would go to another of the neighbors and have another barn dance. We might have two or three of those before hay season came in.

This is what they did for fun, but there was one thing they did not allow. There was no smoking. You know smoking around hay, a simple ash would burn the barn down. There was no smoking, and there wasn't any drinking. I remember them drinking iced tea and cold water because we had a spring house. It was just a time of fun, and it was just a time to have a hoedown.

Now, country folks still do this in some parts of the South down here. They get together, they don't have the old barns like we did up there, but they do get together and they do have hoedowns. At Newborn they do this, but they don't dance, we go and listen to old country music.

I remember that every once in a while one of the band members passed away. They would have the casket in the home, and friends and family would come to the home for the viewing. I can remember that they would hold the viewing mostly in the front room; and as a kid sitting there, I remember seeing these people, old people to me, how old their hands looked as they came pass the casket, and how stooped their shoulders were from the hard work; and it just made an impression upon me of what it was like to be farmers in those days.

I also remember, a fond remembrance of the people who played for these dances in different parts of the country, and of the barn dances at Grandpa's house and Grandma's house. Lucy was a good host. She didn't sing that I know of, but she could sing, and she didn't play.

Grandpa Rocks!

Grandpa played and so she became the hostess and there would be maybe five or six, maybe eight couples, would come bring their instruments. There would be banjos, mandolins, and violins. My aunt Jean played the piano, though she was more of a honky tonk-type pianist. She was probably the best one of the whole group.

They would come and practice songs, new songs and old songs. Every once in a while, they would miss a note, but that didn't make any difference. Everybody would laugh, and they would just go on. I remember at the funerals, when one of them would pass, staring at their old hands that couldn't get their fingers on the strings anymore like they used to. I can see why they would miss a note every now and then, but you know it just didn't make any difference. They were having fun and at a funeral, they were showing love to the one who had passed on. So that's kind of the way it was and Grandpa's violin was in the middle of it. So I grew up enjoying violin music and country music. Now, Grandpa and Grandma passed on. Their farm is now owned by somebody else, but the story of the violin lives on.

Carl Anderson, my cousin, was the son of my aunt Gladys, who was one of Grandpa Duncan's daughters. He had the violin for a number of years, and it had just been setting in the case. Nobody was using it.

At our home in Unity, Ohio, Jean and I are married, had three children, and belonged to an organization called International Students. This organization sponsored foreign students who wanted to come to this country to study. They lived with a sponsor family. So, this is the story of one of those students, from Geneva College.

During the Korean War, the North Koreans had come down into the South Korea and had devastated a lot of the villages. Young's village was devastated and he was captured by the North Koreans. They would take all the young men north. Somewhere along the way the U.S. Air Force was bombing this column. They didn't know there were civilians in it, but they did know there were North Koreans in it. During the bombing in all the confusion, Young and a bunch of others were able to escape from this group of North Koreans, then they started south again. Well, it wasn't long before they ran into the American GIs.

Well, they took him back to the area where he would be safe. They realized that he was good at keeping records and well educated, so they assigned him to a Navy Commander, and he worked in his office. Young came from a wealthy family and had gone through to the highest educational level possible.

His father had four ships that they had used for transportation between Korea and Japan. These four ships has been blown up, and his father's only option was working a menial job in the post office for the Americans. The Commander liked Young and sponsored him to come to the United States.

Young signed up to meet some Americans, especially Christian Americans. Young was a Christian. He was very young, but he was a Christian. So, we got in contact with him and brought him into our home–one of the many times that we did. He stayed in our home on the weekends, and over a period of time he told us that he had played a violin.

Well, I had completely forgot about Grandpa's violin. We found it, my aunt Gladys had it. We worked at getting it restored. Young said that it needed some new strings, so we bought new strings for it. Young went to work to preserve this violin and put the strings on it. Young had worked on it for a weekend, and he asked if he could take it back to Geneva College with him. He put the strings on it and brought it back with him that weekend.

Well, on Sunday morning, Young was always used to getting up very early, praying, reading his Bible and having fellowship with the Lord. One Sunday morning, we heard some of the most melodic sounds coming from downstairs in our living room. I asked Jean if she had left the radio on and she said no. I said listen to that, listen to that. Quietly we came to the head of the stairs and slowly crept downstairs quietly. There was Young, walking from the dining room to the living room, through the kitchen and back again with his eyes half closed. He was playing Grandpa's violin.

Now, in all the years I have never heard that kind of music, because Grandpa had always played the see-saw type of music, and he played it well. He never did know how to play the new modern stuff, but this was classical. Grandpa's violin had the most mellow, the most deep, soothing tone. It was just simply beautiful. We just kind of sat there, Jean and I on the stairs, and just listened to the beautiful music coming out of that old violin. Now, that violin was made in 1727, but it wasn't a Stradivarius, but I'm telling you right now that violin had a Stradivarius sound. It was just simply beautiful. Young met an American girl and married her. They had four children and went back to Korea as missionaries where they now live.

The violin had a hidden secret and quality that I just can't imagine, I never knew that there was that kind of sound that would come out of that violin. I know that Grandpa would never have known it either. In the hands of two masters, the same instrument produced two different yet breathtaking styles of music, it was a blessing and a gift from God.

Three Toes

Three Toes was a black orphaned bear. A few years before I came to Grandpa's farm, there was a black bear mother who had a cub with her and she killed two dogs that were chasing her.

Now, you know that when a bear has a cub, this is not a good place for anyone or anything to be. Grandpa said that when she had her cub with her that she would be really mean, and of course, those two dogs didn't know that.

Three years later, some of the farmers became alarmed when they had found bear tracks in their cornfield, which was close to the pasture where their cattle were feeding. Now, there's always plenty of deer tracks and stuff down there, and there's always berries for deer and other small animals to eat, but when they saw bear tracks they became alarmed.

Some of the farmers decided then to set bear traps hoping to catch both the mother and baby bear. Of course now, the cub had grown up some, and they didn't know how big the cub would be, but it would be big enough to cause problems. Everyone would keep checking when they went to the feed mill for news of the capture of the bears. The farmers even put some money together that would serve as reward money for whoever caught the bears. That was almost four hundred dollars.

Two weeks after the traps were set and after the sighting of the bear tracks in the field, but everyone would keep checking when they went to McRoberts Feed Mill in Enon Valley, Pennsylvania, for any news. In those days, that was quite a large sum to catch two bears. They were going then to bring the bear hide and they were going to nail it onto the side of the feed mill as proof that they got the bear and they would get the four hundred dollars.

When the farmers took their corn and wheat to McRoberts Feed Mill, they carried their guns with them just in case they might trap that bear. I can remember seeing Grandpa's gun as I rode with him to the feed mill on a number of occasions, but we never did see that bear. I was kind of glad about that, really. But, you know what?

One of those farmers caught something in one of those traps. There were three bear toes. They didn't know which bear the toes belonged to. The farmer who caught three bear toes, thought he ought to have some of the reward money.

Now even Christian farmers can and do have a difference of opinions, and at the feed mill that day when they brought in them three toes, this was the situation. This difference of opinions resulted in quite an argument. The big argument arose since the farmer had caught some of the bear, he thought he ought to have some of the money. It made pretty good sense. The owner of the feed mill was a wise man, he gave the farmer, one bag of ground corn for each toe, so he got three sacks in all. Plus, ten sacks would be there for the time when the rest of the bear was nailed on the wall of the feed mill. Well, that settled the argument. It was fair, and everyone seemed to agree to it. Mr. McRoberts nailed those three toes on the side of the feed mill for all to see, and they are there to this day.

That summer at Grandpa's farm, it was another summer night and we were sitting on the front porch just listening to the tree frogs, the hoot owl and someone's dog way out in the distance. He's a coon hunter. You could hear the dog howl. It's a warm summer night about 11:30 p.m. Grandma was swinging back and forth on the porch swing, and the swing was making its special sound. Grandpa was smoking his corncob pipe, sitting in his rocking chair, and it was making its special sound. Each time he went back and forth on the rocker, it squeaked, smoke floating all over the porch. Old Blue, the hunting dog, was laying at Grandpa's feet sound asleep.

Grandpa said, "You know, at the end of a hard day's work, what else would anybody want? My honey is on the swing, my coon dog is at my feet. I'm sitting in my favorite chair. I'm smoking my pipe, and I have my grandson to help me on the farm. What else could anybody want?"

I want to tell you, I felt ten feet tall. My chest bunched up. My grandpa needed me. Wow. What else could anybody want?

On a still summer night the smallest sound can be heard. Even the bats, when they're flying catching bugs, you can hear the flapping of their wings. It seems to me that the night must be a special night.

Grandma broke the silence. "Did you hear that sound?"

Grandpa said, "No."

Now, Grandpa was a bit hard of hearing, and he would never admit it. Old Blue's one ear come up and then laid back down very quiet.

"Grandpa, I hear something out there behind the barn, " Grandma persisted.

"I don't hear anything."

Old Blue's big ears came up and he started to sniff, then was real quiet again.

"Grandpa there's something loose behind that barn!" Grandma exclaimed.

Old Blue's ears were standing straight up now, and he started to growl. Sam reached for his gun by the door and he said to Blue, "Heel."

The moon came up from behind the clouds and lit up the whole barnyard, and then we heard that noise again. Even Grandpa heard it this time. With his gun in his hand, Old Blue beside him, and me right behind him Grandpa took a step. Then Old Blue took a step, and then I took a step. My hair started standing straight up on the back of my neck and my skin was cold all over. We all three take steps in unison across the barnyard. We finally got to the corner of the barn and that noise was louder than ever before. All of my hair was standing straight up. Suddenly I smelled wet rugs that had been laying there for a long, long time. What an awful smell.

Grandpa turned to me and said, "Three Toes, Three Toes."

Grandpa Rocks!

Old Blue wanted to get a bite of that bear's behind, but Sam said, "Heel, Blue. Heel, Blue."

Old Three Toes was so busy getting into that beehive and eating honey, he didn't hear us coming up behind him. Sam pulled the hammer back on the gun, both barrels, pointed it right at old Three Toes' backside, and pulled the trigger.

Grandpa fell back from the shock of the gun and said to Blue, "Sic 'em!" Old Blue got a big mouthful of that bear's behind.

Now old Three Toes came straight into the air with one big howl, three sections of that beehive hanging down on his neck. He went straight into the air, took off flat up over the hill with Old Blue just chomping at his backside. Just before he went over the hill, Grandpa shot both barrels once again. Old Blue come back with that bear's tail and a mouthful of flesh. There was a big hunk of meat.

Now, Grandma was on the front porch calling instructions the whole time. Grandpa and I were so scared, we weren't even listening. My hair finally laid back down on my head, and my heart was pounding.

You know, being on Grandpa's farm, it's sure a lot of fun.

The next day, we went to Enon Valley to the feed mill with that bear tail and a piece of the hide. Sam nailed it alongside of those three toes, and it's still there today. Grandpa got three sacks of ground corn.

The moral to this story is: If you've got your head down, and you are doing something you shouldn't be , don't stick your behind up because somebody's just liable to kick it.

MOUNT JACKSON'S GUARDIAN ANGEL

All my friends had cars. We were always washing and Simonizing them, and of course, bragging about how fast they would go! We did talk about girls some, but our cars were the center of our conversations!

Since we lived in the farm country, the roads were not crowded. It was always "Hi ho, Silver, and away we would go!"

On Sunday night after Young People's Meeting, we would decide to go to an ice cream shop that was in the next town. Girls and guys would pile into our cars and off we would go, spinning out of the parking lot of the church. We never thought about wearing out our tires!

We were on our way for root beer sodas or whatever they wanted! The last driver there had to buy the first driver there a root beer soda! All I can say is that I didn't buy many root beer sodas! We were having good Christian fun! I didn't say it was always well-thought out or safe!

Robert Huston

In all those growing up years no one ever got hurt! I believe we kept God's angels busy. I'm sure it is written down in the libraries of Heaven. I write the previous so you would have a better understanding of what is next.

A couple of months later, two of my friends and I were in a little town called Mahoningtown at one of their pool halls. We had been there about four hours, and it was closing time. Someone made the remark, "I can get to Mount Jackson square before you can."

Mount Jackson was about fifteen miles away. We all made for the door and ran to our cars! My car was across the street and heading out of town toward Mount Jackson. The other cars were heading the wrong way, and they had to turn around. That gave me a head start and I had gotten through the bridge and started up the long hill when they caught up. I stayed in the middle of the road, but they finally passed me and were pulling away. When we got to the top of the hill they were five car lengths ahead of me.

Now something happened! I pushed my gas pedal to the floor. Me and that 1936 Ford started to catch up. By the time we were outside of Mount Jackson, we were three abreast, on a two lane road!

I was on the left side, and my one friend was driving a new black Chevy V8. He was in the middle. My other friend was driving on the right side in a new Chrysler. We came to the square, bumper to bumper. No one was going to give in! That's when it happened!

There was someone on the top of the hill, coming at us from the opposite direction, barreling straight at us on my side of the road. Six head lights were shining on him. You could see the driver freeze, continuing straight toward us. His eyes were as big as "dinner plates!" I'm sure his life passed before him. There wasn't time for anything else! We were all three doing around eighty miles per hour coming into that crossroads. . . one innocent victim and three foolish young men!

The black Chevy went straight down over the hill and had a hard time stopping! He turned around and came back to the crossroads expecting to find three dead people and a pile of junk on fire. There was nothing, everything was very quiet! What happened?

I had made a hard left and was looking at the country store. I should have gone clear through it and out the backside, but there was a little hill in front of the store and my car went up that rise and back to the left across the road. I went back and forth across that road for quite a ways. When I stopped, I sat there shaking for some time. After calming down some, I gingerly drove back to the square expecting to find dead people and junk. All I saw was my friend and that black Chevy. Where was my other friend in the Chrysler?

We went looking for him and found him in the Mount Jackson High School parking lot with his head down on the steering wheel. He had made a hard right at eighty at the square and almost had taken the porch off of a house. Crossing the road, he barely missed a porch of the facing house. He went through yards and flower beds, and eventually spun out in the school parking lot.

He thought he had died and gone to heaven, and he hadn't said good-bye to his mom. He sat there crying with his head down on the wheel. When we tapped on the window he thought we were angels and wouldn't open his window for some time! We all made a vow that night!

No more racing and never tell anyone what had happened.

In my teenage years, I did not trust God at all. I thought he was completely unfair. You see I had a cousin that was just married to a wonderful fellow, they were very happy. Three months into their happy married life, she contracted polio. It settled into her lungs and throat. Even though she was in an iron lung, she choked to death! I had no one to council me, so from that time on I had no time for God!

It wasn't until a few years later, with the experience I had with the Eighth Air Force. While overseas a loving God showed Himself to me, and the Holy Spirit drew me in and I discovered that He was a God of Love and Perfection!

At twenty six years of age, I asked the Lord, who I had never trusted, to come into my heart. I gave him my mind and all I had and He did something amazing in a dream. He showed me this story in all the vivid details in a dream.

He showed me how one of his angels stood in Mount Jackson square and with his hands had turned one car right, and one car left, allowing the other to go straight ahead, sparing all of our lives! If I hadn't lived it, I wouldn't have believed it!

SLIPPERY FINGERS

Where I grew up there was this kid and his name was Dutch. Dutch had a dream of becoming a famous ball player. He saved all the cards, knew all the heroes, he had his own ball glove and a special hat. He even had a uniform and on the back was the name, Dizzy Dean, after an old pitcher.

Dutch wanted to be just like Dizzy Dean. He wanted to be a ball player. The kids wouldn't let Dutch play very

often, especially on the bases. You know why they wouldn't let Dutch play? Every time the ball would come to him, and he knew it was going to come, he would blink. There is no way you can catch a ball with your eyes closed. So they nicknamed him Slippery Fingers.

The kids didn't treat Slippery Fingers very well. When they would pick up sides, guess who was chosen last? Slippery Fingers. They would never put him on bases, he was always way out in the field, right field. What Slippery Fingers did have was a good arm and he could really rifle a ball in. Slippery Fingers wanted to be Dizzy Dean on the bases, but the kids didn't know that.

Slippery Fingers went to high school. He didn't go out for sports because of his nervous blink. He did try out for the cheerleading squad and became a cheerleader. He became president of his high school class the freshman year, the sophomore year, and the junior year.

Now, Slippery Fingers had a nervous blink, but God gave him something he didn't know that he had. He had leadership qualities and speaking qualities. He became president of the FFA, Future Farmers of America, and other organizations that needed leadership qualities as he grew up in high school. In his senior year, he signed up for the service.

The story of Slippery Fingers is very personal to me. Be very careful how you label each other, we don't all have the same abilities, and until we find ourselves our fellow man should just stand there and be supportive. I was Slippery Fingers.

HARVEST TIME

Dad was the foreman of the Kelso ranch and farm for seventeen years or so. This is where I grew up. One of my most memorial times of the year is about the time that the oats and wheat were ready for harvest. These are wonderful memories to go along with this time of year.

There was a man who had an old steam engine tractor with big wire wheels. This tractor only traveled about eight miles an hour. When he blew the air whistle, you knew that harvest time had come to the Kelso farm. He rented his thrashing machine to each farmer as their crops came due.

We had cut the oats and wheat with a binder and had shocked the fields. "Shocking the fields" is when you take sheaves of wheat and stack them together in bundles of twenty-one to be later picked up in a wagon and hauled to the thrashing machine.

I should explain what a thrashing machine looks like. In the front was a hopper where you pitched the sheaves from the wagon into that hopper. The fingered rollers pull the wheat sheaves into the machine. Then the sheaves would go into the shakers inside the thrasher that separated the wheat or oats from the stock. The wheat would go down the chutes into a burlap sack that was tied and carried into the granary in the barn. The straw was blown out the chute at the other end of a long extension, forming a straw stack.

That steam engine had a large pulley on its side that connected a long belt to the thrashing machine which ran at a high rate of speed. This was the way the thrashing machine got its power to work! This thrashing machine was owned by all the farmers, sort of like a co-op. The steam engine guy kept the repairs up.

On the morning of the thrashing, eight to ten neighbors with their wagons and teams would show up at our farm. They would stay and help until all the harvesting was done. It might be two or three days. Then we would go to their farms and do the same thing. It was called neighboring.

A thrashing machine, when it was running, was really noisy and when a team of horses pulled up along side with a wagon load of wheat sheaves, they acted a little skittish. The horse closest to the hopper of the machine would have the hairs of their mane braided. Their tails would also have to be hobbed to stay clear of the pulleys of the machine. I only know of one time that these pulleys became a problem! It happened at our farm.

One of our neighbors had pulled his team along side and began to pitch wheat sheaves into the hopper. When the inside horse moved sideways, close to the thrasher, his tail got caught in one of those pulleys. It started to wrap around it. Total panic broke out. There was no instant brake that could be pulled. The machine had to coast to a stop. By that time, the horse had lost its tail. What a mess. You can make your own picture!

Let's talk about some wonderful memories of the thrashing season. When all the neighbor's came together, so did the best cooks. If you have ever tasted farm cooking, you know what I am talking about!

Mashed potatoes piled high with dark gravy on them. Fresh sweet corn, green beans, peas, pickled beets, tomatoes fixed in some fashion, lime pickles, and some green onions, homemade bread, butter, apple butter, plum jam and the best home-raised beef and pork.

The best was yet to come. The desserts: The pies, elderberry, red raspberry, cherry, apple, and peach. If you had time and the appetite, you could have more than one piece. The smell of all that food to share with neighbors was the time to say "Thank you, Lord, for all these blessings," which we did every day in our own homes!

Everyone was hot and sweaty. When the dinner bell sounded, all would meet at the Kelso house. Someone would be at the outside pitcher pump filling up large basins with water, that rested on a long wooden bench. Everyone took off their shirts and started splashing themselves with this water. Before long there was a wet towel fight and water fight, all in fun. Sometimes a wrestling match ensued. Everyone would then grab basin of water and threw it on the guys who were wrestling.

The women would get irritated because the food was on the table and these men were acting like boys!

Robert Huston

Somebody would ring the bell again, then everyone would rush to the table, pushing and shoving for the best seats. The blessing was said, the food was passed, but the fun wasn't over yet. There was much conversation around the table. When someone was talking and looking the other way, and the butter was being passed, the one passing the butter would shove it into his thumb and everyone would laugh!

Another thing they would do when it was time for dessert, this has always been my special part of the meal. You really had to watch your pie! If you turned your head, someone would switch plates on you; sometimes take a large bite out of your piece, but the funniest thing I ever saw was pulled on a man named Charlie. He had a piece of peach pie in front of him and the man on his left side engaged him in a political argument. Charlie wasn't watching his pie. The fellow on his right side took a big scoop of mustard out of the dish and lifted the top crust of Charlie's pie and put the mustard in the pie and laid the crust back down. That same person started to thank the ladies for how good that pie was and started eating his own pie. Of course, Charlie didn't want to be left out, he took his first bite. You should have seen the look on his face! He knew he had been snickered but he didn't let on. With every bite he would praise the cooks and take a big gulp of water. Everyone roared. By this time, he was really sweating and his face was red!

Farm work was hard, but we had fun.

GHOST STORY

This story begins down on the farm of Sam Duncan, who happens to be my grandpa. It will be the first time that I will be living down on the farm, and my age will be around eight years old.

This was going to be a very exciting time, there were so many wonderful things to see and learn, at this time. I didn't even know what chores meant, and I had not experienced my grandma's cooking yet.

We were sitting on the front porch about 11:00 at night; Grandpa in his favorite rocking chair smoking his pipe, Grandma sitting on the swing as usual, the night was very, very quiet.

Grandpa said, "May I tell you a story?"

I said, "Sure, I like stories."

Grandma said, "Now, Sam, don't you tell the young boy a whopper, wait till he's old enough, eight years old, he can stand a little bit of scary stuff."

Grandpa took out his watch and looked at it, it was about 11:30 and he said, "One time years ago at this time, there was a ghost train came down those tracks that ran through Enon valley. It was just like a night like this when it was a real still, there was no schedule of a train to run at 11:30 at night, but the whistle was heard and the train was coming down the tracks. There was a railroad worker coming up the tracks that night. He didn't hear the ghost train coming. The next morning, he was found dead on the tracks, apparently he was hit by the ghost train. To this very day, no one knows for sure how he died when everyone in town said it must be the ghost train."

Now Grandpa said, "I have lived here for a number of years and haven't seen nor heard the ghost train, but I believe that story.

"So when I go to sleep tonight, I just might hear the whistle of that ghost train, and if it comes through at 12:00 tonight, it'll probably shake the room that I'm going to be sleeping in."

Grandma said, "Now that's enough of that, you've scared the boy half to death."

Now I was told this story when I was eight years old and over the years I kind of forgot about it. Now I was now sitting on the porch at about 11:30 at night, and I was now twelve years old. All of the sudden I heard a train whistle. Grandpa looked at his watch and said, "There shouldn't be a train running at this time of night," and proceeded to put his watch back in his pocket.

I looked across the country, it was very, very dark, and I heard the train whistle once again. When I looked at Grandpa, Grandma, and the dog, they were all in suspended animation. Grandpa was in the possession of blowing smoke out of his mouth. Grandma's knitting needles were falling off her lap and were hanging in the air suspended. The dog's ears started coming up and were just hanging there. I looked across the country again and heard the train whistle. I looked back at my grandparents, and they were still in suspended animation. The hair was standing up on the back of my neck, maybe Grandpa's story he told me when I was eight years old was true.

All of the sudden, I got cold all over, and I didn't know really what to do. Grandpa and Grandma sure weren't going to help me. I'd just sat there froze and looking across country. I couldn't, the train was getting closer and closer and closer, and the whistle was getting louder and louder and louder. It was five minutes till twelve, and at 12:00 the whistle and train went away.

When I was watching the train in night, I could see somebody standing on the tracks trying to flag the train down. I wondered if that person was a ghost too. You know the next day they did find someone that had been on the tracks that night and was hit by a train, but there was no train scheduled at 12:00.

At 12:01, I looked at my grandpa and grandma again. She caught the knitting needles with one hand, Grandpa continued to blow smoke out of his mouth, and the dog let out a growl.

What was I to do? Should I say something?

I didn't think they would believe me, so the whole time I was down on the farm, I never told anybody the story. Would you have believed me?

Twenty years later, I was still bothered by this story and what I saw that night. What bothered me most of all was the lantern the ghost man was swinging to stop the ghost train; it must be on the tracks someplace. One day, when I was in Enon Valley, I didn't tell anybody what I was going to do. I took a walk down those tracks about a mile to where I saw the light to go straying and looked for the ghost man's lantern.

We did bury him twenty years ago, but nobody ever thought about his light. I was going to try to find it to see if I really saw a ghost train. It took me about an hour to get down to where I thought the light should be. It took me another hour searching in the weeds to find the light, and what I'm going to tell you, you won't believe. Down in the weeds was an old rusted lantern, and we've just got the top and the handle of the ghost light.

Even though I found the light twenty years later, I still could not tell anybody because they would not have believed me.

Do you believe in ghosts? I do, but please don't tell anybody. They won't believe you either, I hope you enjoyed this story.

ONE-EYED SAM

Horace Samuel Henderson, III, was an old-fashioned country preacher. The kids had nicknamed him One-Eyed Sam, and that is how he was known by the people. He had a Bible in one hand, an old trumpet around his neck, and he rode a big light tan mule called Zeb.

Now, I want to explain to you a little bit about "hollers." In northern Pennsylvania, it is called a "hollow." In Israel, it's called a "wadi." In southern Pennsylvania and Ohio, it's called a "holler." It means a valley between two hills and in this holler lived the Huston clan. . . my clan.

Now, there were the mountain Hustons, the lowland Hustons, and the redheaded Hustons. They all kept pretty much to themselves and didn't interact. The mountain Hustons were the timber people, and they also had trained dogs that hunted bear and coon. The lowland Hustons were the farmers and the sharp business people. The redheaded Hustons lived miles up the holler. They raised fighting roosters and were carpenters.

Now, the mountain Hustons and the redheaded Hustons had something in common, they both had stills. The mountain Hustons made moonshine from corn squeezings called White Lightning. The redheaded Hustons made hooch out of berry squeezings. The lowland Hustons had the country store, and that was my grandfather and grandmother's store. Grandpa did business with all the Hustons in the holler.

Now, Grandma didn't like the idea of Grandpa buying hooch and moonshine and selling it in the store, but it was good for business. Grandpa had a special room in the back, way in the back, which he kept locked, but everybody knew it was there. The country store was on the edge of the lowland Hustons' territory. Even though all the Hustons in the other clans didn't like each other, they all came to the country store to do business. Grandpa and the drinking Hustons had a signal. When they were ready to buy a jug, they would run their fingers across the rim of their hat, and then they would sneak into the back of the store.

Grandma kept a jug of berry hooch up in the cupboard to be used only for colds and upset stomachs. Oh, did I tell you? She put some in the vegetable soup and some of her other cooking too. She'd put in what we'd call a jigger, which is as much as you can pour in with a good snap of the wrist. Then she would let the jug set on the counter while she went to the henhouse to gather up some eggs.

While she was gone, Grandpa would sneak into the kitchen and he would taste the hooch, he said, "Just to see if it was all right." Then he would put two more jiggers into the soup. So that was three jiggers. Now, One-Eyed Sam never drank. But he loved Grandma's cooking and came often just for a bowl of her vegetable soup.

One-Eyed Sam always had a place to stay. He would go from Huston to Huston to sleep and eat; reading the Bible to them and telling them many stories, and, he could laugh. Oh my, could he laugh.

Sam also had a temper that you didn't want to get him riled. Everyone knew that, and that is how he got his name, "One-Eyed Sam?" When he got excited, his one eyelid started flickering and, his other eye would bulge out, and it wasn't good to be around Sam when his eye bulged out.

Now, One-eyed Sam came to dinner at our house quite often. I want you to understand that Sam never drank, and his message was, "Repent, or go to hell."

One-Eyed Sam held his first camp meeting in Huston Holler at Grandpa's country store. It was the only time that all the Hustons were together. Sam was the only one they all liked. First, there were four or five self-appointed preachers who would preach for two hours, and then One-Eyed Sam took center stage.

His eye started blinking. Holding a Bible in one hand and with a two-edged sword out of his mouth, he pounced back and forth on the porch of the store. Getting excited he would throw his coat down and stand on his toes. His one eye began to bulge and the Holy Spirit came down, and it was like a cloud falling on Huston Holler. One lady filled with the Spirit jumped up and said, "Martha, I'm the one who said you were skinny dipping in the creek with Mark."

Then Martha, filled with the Holy Spirit jumped up and said, "It wasn't Mark, it was Ben." One of the mountain Hustons said that he had stolen a cow from one of the lowland Hustons years ago and started the rumor that a bear must have gotten it. He asked forgiveness, pulled out a wad of money and paid three times what the cow was worth.

It was exciting, confessing, hugging, and forgiving. I have never seen the Hustons do that. Some stood up and announced, "I will burn my still." One right after another did this.

One-Eyed Sam's eye was bulging and he was screaming, "Repent, you sinners. . . " The mountain Hustons, the lowland Hustons, the redheaded Hustons, started to love one another.

One-Eye Sam hadn't been seen for some time. Grandma started putting more pies out to cool, knowing that Sam would suddenly show up, but he hadn't for a long time. His mule, Zeb, was found down in the pasture by the creek, the saddle and the halter hung on the gate. Sam would never have left his mule. We couldn't find him, and we walked all over the holler. It was decided that he had been taken up in God's Chariot, his body was never found.

Well, Zeb, now has died and a cross has been erected in the field. Huston Holler is still a good place to live. Horace Samuel Henderson, III, has not been forgotten. A large stone with writing on it was placed at the country store and it says this: To the man of God who wasn't afraid to preach the truth where it was surely needed. Amen.

PULLING CONTEST

My grandpa's farm was at the end of the Appalachian Mountain Range in western Pennsylvania. Most of the good fields were on top of these ranges. South of the farm we had lots of timber, mostly hardwood. Grandpa allowed some of that to be cut out. The logger had a team of horses, but Grandpa used his mule team also. He wanted to keep watch on what trees were being cut out. Both teams pulled these logs out to the main road to be loaded over the next four weeks.

Mr. Welder, the logger, said, "Sam, these mules can out pull my team all day long, Canfield is coming up. Why don't you enter your mules in the pulling contest? I think they can win."

Grandpa and Grandma talked this idea over for a week. Mr. Welder offered to haul the team to the fair free for him. So that is how Knucklehead, Bess and all our family got to the Canfield Fair in eastern Ohio.

Once Grandpa had gotten there, he wished he had stayed on the farm. He saw some of the best horse flesh in Ohio and Pennsylvania. They all had new harnesses, with brass and silver on them. Some of the horses owners were making fun of Grandpa's mule team, but it wasn't mean fun! They thought Grandpa's team was outclassed, Grandpa thought so too.

The next morning the pulling contest started. A pulling contest is putting chunks of iron slabs on a metal sled and pulling it for a specified distance. The heavy weights went first, and it was great to see those teams lean into it with all their rippling muscles, trying to move it as far as they could.

Right after dinner the middle-weights began. That was Grandpa's category. All afternoon one team after another pulled their best sled, extra weight was added and gradually teams were eliminated as the weight was added.

Low and behold, there was three teams left for a final pull. Guess whose these teams were! One was a set of blacks from southern Ohio, who had won many pull-offs. The next was a beautiful team of apple-grays from Harrisburg, Pennsylvania, followed by a team of mules that just happened to belong to Grandpa Sam!

The pull-off contest people put more pig-iron slabs on the sled. The announcer said, "This is more weight than has ever been pulled at this level."

The apple-grays were first. They hooked them up and the driver picked up the lines and said, "Haw." The horses snapped and dirt flew. They moved that sled one third of the way! The crowd in the grandstand went wild and the team stopped. The driver calmed his team down and again picked up the reigns and said, "Haw." They moved it to the halfway mark and stopped. They had done their best!

Grandpa Rocks!

The team of blacks was next, they were hooked up. The driver said, "Haw." At first they didn't pull together, then they started to dig in and pulled that sled one half of the way and stopped. On the second try they got the sleigh three feet from the end and could go no more. They were finished.

Everything was very, very quiet as Grandpa led his big brown mule team up to the sled. Here was a team that wasn't supposed to be here, and now they were in the pull of their lives. Grandpa's jaw was set, his eyes were riveted on the finish line! He had the lines in his hands. When the hook snapped onto the sled, Grandpa yelled, "Get, dig dig."

Those mules, Knucklehead and Bess, started to dig. At first nothing happened, and then the sled came up and started to move. On the first pull, they had pulled one inch over halfway. The people in the stands and the officials, even the drivers of the other teams, were now behind Grandpa's mule team.

Grandpa dropped the lines and walked up in front of the mules, rubbing their noses, he spoke softly, "You are the best mule team there ever was. If we don't make it, it's okay, but let's show these horses who is 'King of the Hill'."

He took his hat off and with his handkerchief he wiped the sweat off his forehead, then he reached down into his pocket and gave each mule a lump of sugar. A thousand eyes were watching Grandpa and the mules. You could hear a pin drop. He went back, picking up those lines once more, he yelled, "Dig, dig!"

Those mules came to life and they started to dig, with their noses almost to the ground. The sled began to move.

The other drivers started yelling, "Dig, dig!"

All the people in the stands started yelling, "Dig, dig!"

Grandpa, in all the excitement lost exactly where the finish line was, but he stopped those mules when he thought they had pulled enough. There was dead silence once again as the judges came out and measured how far the sled was pulled. The distance was one foot more than the finish line.

The crowd went wild. Grandpa walked up to Knucklehead and Bess, wrapping his arms around their necks and stood there crying. I had never seen Grandpa do that before. Our whole family was in tears and joyful at the same time. Sam got a blue ribbon for the team, and a blue ribbon for the best team driver.

The newspaper in Pennsylvania and Ohio had taken photos of that pull and wrote about the miracle team of mules owned by Sam Duncan in western Pennsylvania. A man of means came up to Grandpa that week and wanted him to take his team to all the county fairs around. He would supply a horse trailer and a new set of harnesses, plus some of the expense money. Grandpa talked it over with Grandma. He felt honored to be asked to do this. But he said, "No." His team had pulled their hearts out for him, and that was enough for him.

In Knucklehead and Bess's stall in Pennsylvania hangs two blue ribbons to this day, for all to see.

How To Buy A Car, Etc.

Well, when Jean and I were very young Christians, we had a very little bit of money, God worked a miracle. I didn't have a spare and the tires on my car were on the tired side of things. One tire was in really bad shape, there was no tread in the middle, but there was still some rubber left on it. Since I was low on money, I thought I could squeeze just a few miles out of that whole set of tires.

We had become part of a Bible Presbyterian Church in the little town of Enon Valley. At that time the Lord was showing and teaching Jean and I to depend on Him, even for the little things. Wouldn't you know, about this time the Women's Missionary Society was having a conference about one hundred and fifty miles from our church.

Jean, my wife, being the good woman that she is offered our car to haul six women to that conference. When she told me what she had done, I went to pray and asked God if He would reconsider and consecrate that car, and please, please, please consecrate those tires.

I didn't say anything to Jean about the tires, but my instructions to Jean were please drive slow and watch out for potholes in the road. The day of the conference finally came and all the women were excited, even Jean. Again, I got God off to the side and reminded him how I had given my life, my car, my powers to His care. I told Him that I believed Him when He said He will take care of little things, and I expected Him to come through. Jean is a good, safe driver, but I know when you get six excited women in a consecrated car and everybody's talking at once, and they never look at the speedometer. You drive by feel.

The Lord did not let me down. Jean had driven about fifty to sixty miles an hour. Everyone had a Christian renewal, and those tired tires brought those women home safe. But where is the miracle? The best is yet to come.

The next day a man at work had a used tire, my size for my car, and sold it to me at a reduced rate, but where was the miracle? I took the tire off the car, broke it down off the rim and let out the air. Removed the tire off the rim and took out the tube and laid it on the garage floor. That little bit of rubber that was on the middle of the tire was gone completely and the whole way around it was an empty shell. I picked up the tube and there was a six inch break in it. On closer examination, I found three pinholes in it and on the other side, another pinhole. That tube had a six inch slit, four pinholes in it, and it didn't leak air until I broke the bead. God had kept His promise to a couple of young Christians and had showed them a miracle in little things.

Grandpa Rocks!

Another time God helped us buy a car. Jean and I were very young in the Lord at that time. We had learned to obey God when He was leading us. We had bought a car and it just had a new paint job and a new engine in it, so we thought we had a great deal. The salesman said that he would sell it to his own mother with a clear conscience. I found out later his mother had already died. That statement came back to me one Sunday morning when we were all loaded for church. We started to back out of my drive when the front seat fell right through the floor. What would have happened at fifty miles an hour with a baby on my wife's lap, while we were on the road to the church? I was mad at myself for being so gullible, and then God took over and entered my mind and said, "Well, Bob, I stopped you while you were still in the drive, didn't I?" Then He made a promise. "I've got something better for you."

That week we sat down with pencil and paper and asked God to lead us to a car that would be in our price range. We wrote down our description: gray, with four doors, low mileage, six cylinders, four good tires, and comparatively new. Now, that's a big order, but not for God Who controls little things.

We waited and nothing happened for six days, but on the seventh day, God's day, I got a call from the dealer who said he had just the car we were looking for. Now, we had been down at different dealers and said this is what we want. So this is why the call came. One thing for sure, we didn't want a car they would sell to the dealer's mother. To make a long story short, we had a car with all our wishes that we had listed and the price was a little higher. We haggled and got it down to what we could afford. Needless to say, we bought the car and fell in love with it immediately. And thanked God.

I'm going to tell you another story that happened about buying a car. This was in 2001 here in Georgia. We have a missionary that is going to Bosnia, and he's been over there trying to start a church. One night, at one of our prayer meetings this missionary said that he had just gotten an e-mail from a friend over in Bosnia and the motor in their car that had just blown out and it wasn't worth fixing. They needed an automobile.

So he made this request, and I said, in my prayer, "Let's pray for a new car. Let's pray for a car at the right price. Let's pray for a car that's got four good tires, has 4-wheel drive since that's mountain country. A car that would get good gas mileage and preferably a diesel." So we prayed for that.

Harry went back over to Bosnia about two to three months later. The man still didn't have a car. What he did have was some medical problems that couldn't be fixed there in Bosnia, so he had to go to Greece to the hospital. When he went to Greece to get this operation done, he spoke to a Christian church there, and told those people that he had a blown engine in his car and that he needed a new car.

The people in Greece had listened to this missionary and had decided to get two or three congregations together and bought this man a car. When he got out of the hospital, he drove that car home. It was a diesel, it had low mileage, 4-wheel drive, and it was the right price and it had not only a heater, but it had a good air conditioning system in it.

Grandpa Rocks!

Now, he knew nothing of the prayer meeting we had here in Georgia. The people in Greece knew nothing of the prayer we had made. They knew of the missionary's request. When Harry came back to the meeting, he had an e-mail and this note.

> Thank you, brother in Christ. I have just received a car and I have brought it home from Greece and back to Bosnia.

Harry then e-mailed back and told this man we had prayed for this in Georgia six months before. Now, God worked it all out.

My First Car

Living on a farm in Pennsylvania was a good place to grow up, but money was tight and my dad only made seventeen dollars a week. We got a home free, all our meat and garden veggies and fruit free also. The farm also had an eighteen or twenty acre fruit orchard. The farm was a good place to raise 4-H pigs, chickens, and strawberries. As you can see we didn't have a lot of luxuries, but we had enough to eat and a good shelter over our heads. But we were poor and didn't know it.

At the time Dad owned a Model A Ford. It was slowly wearing out. He had been saving to buy a new "Chevy" for the last four years. The day came when his new "Chevy" came in. He let me go with him to pick it up, taking the Model A for one last run at fifty miles per hour down the road. I was getting close to driving age, and I was excited, thinking Dad would share his new car with me! I would wash and polish it for him, but no sharing, at least not for now!

The day came when my mother had a long talk with Dad on my behalf. After that came the rules of how to drive that new "Chevy." There was to be no speeding, no more than two kids at one time, whatever gas was used had to be replaced, check the tires, the oil and the water and be home before twelve. Good heavens, after that, I hated to even ask to use his car. I did once in a while, but when I got home my dad would check the mileage and the tires for how hot they were, also the engine. He would then check for any scratches on the car. It got so bad that when I did get the car, I would drive to one of my friends' homes and leave the car there. I would ride with them and help buy their gas. At sixteen and seventeen I had a hard time trying to understand my dad's attitude about his car. Only, after years later, did I even come close to understanding his concern for his car.

It became evident that the sooner I bought my own car that this problem could be solved. The word went out, all of my friends and their dads were looking for a car for me. The car dealership where Dad bought the "Chevy" had some, but they were all big cars and I wanted a smaller one. One of my friends had a cousin who lived in South Carolina had a 1936 Ford coupe, dark green and wanted to sell it for three hundred and fifty dollars. My heart jumped. His cousin was coming up for a visit in three weeks. They would bring it along, I had saved three hundred dollars. As you can see I was a little short. One of the farmers that sold produce said that he would loan me that fifty dollars I needed and use my strawberry patch as collateral. Three weeks later I had my first car. What an exciting day!

Two things I should tell you about that Ford, the first is that the brakes you had to adjust by hand, one wheel at a time. My car had the habit of pulling to the left when you applied the brakes. I was getting ready for an education on how to be a problem solver.

Jacking up the left front, I then crawled underneath, while looking at the backside of the wheel I saw two lugs sticking out. They were the brake adjustment. I needed to turn those lugs to the left and right. The brake shoes would move out against the wheel drum so you would have brakes when they were applied. On this front wheel only one shoe was working, the other shoes froze up.

I took an open ended wrench and tried to move the lugs. They were really tight. I had to spray each with penetrating oil and let it stand for thirty minutes and then try it again. I had to go over all four wheels in this manner.

What you had to do was take the open-ended wrench and turn the one lug to the left until the shoes were tight against the brake drum and then back it off a smidgen just so it didn't drag. Then you would turn the others to the right and back it off a smidgen. I would go down the road a half mile going through all the gears to get the speed up to fifty miles an hour then apply the brakes. When you had all four brakes sliding together, you had it just right. On a wet day sometimes they would get out of adjustment. You never knew which one was going to grab first! I went into pin wheels a number of times. It was fun. What fond memories I have.

The second was that there was a leak at the corner of the windshield. I tried to fix that but never was sure it was fixed. So I would go down the road and do a sharp right and then a sharp left. That move would empty all the water underneath the dash. It worked pretty well. On prom night I had not turned right and left hard enough. There was still rusty water underneath the dash.

I picked up my date with her new prom dress and shoes. When I turned into the school where the prom was the water spilled out on her dress and ran down into her new shoes. I think she was a bit perturbed because she never gave me one dance and she asked one of my friends to take her home. So much for flowers and proms. I had even adjusted the brakes and polished the car!

Fixing Fence

On a farm you are always cutting fence posts, mending fence, digging postholes, or stretching wire. With all the other chores, when do you have time to fix fences? Well, there is an answer to that question, you wait until it looks like rain. As the clouds start rolling in, that is when you get the stone boat out, put six fence posts on it, some barbed wire, staples, posthole diggers, and a barbed-wire puller. You also need some wire for wrapping around the posts. Also needed are a sledge, an axe, a specially built hammer to drive and pull staples.

Off you go! It always seems like you are going to the farthest end of the farm and that the cattle always found the weakest spot in the fence. You can never chase an animal back through the same hole he went out through, you always have to chase them back in through the main gate.

It sure looks like rain! So there we were stretching wire and fixing the fence when the rain clouds start rolling in. We were going to get soaked. We always got soaked! That was the way it was on Grandpa's farm.

After a while I enjoyed getting soaked from the rain. It was better than sweating yourself wet.

We had been fixing fence a while when we first saw the bear tracks. Two sets, one little, and one big. Grandpa carried a loaded gun with him. Grandpa said, "Let's not worry Grandma just yet. She has enough on her mind these days, with the fox getting into the hen house and the hawk carrying away her pet chicken. Also the heavy rain that washed out her early garden."

That's when we heard a noise coming from the swamp. Grandpa said, "We better ease out of here."

When we got back to the farm, soaking wet, Grandpa called one of our neighbors from the shed. The alert was out. One phone call is all it takes on a party line. Of course, Grandma picked up the phone and was listening in.

When we went to the house to change clothes, it started.

"Why didn't you tell me about that bear? Don't we have enough to worry about? You told everyone else! Why not me? Don't you think I should know!"

Now I knew Grandpa loved Grandma, but it is very hard at age twelve to sort these things out.

CAR BASEBALL

What a blessing to own your own car! It gives you power on the road, the ability to come and go at will, Gas was always a problem! I didn't have a lot of money at any time. It kind of trickled in through many various ways. I sold my 4-H strawberries at market, sold my pigs, dozens of eggs to people, and sometimes from helping Grandpa on his farm. I was a young guy who liked being on the go, liked having fun, and needed gasoline for my car.

I was good friends with one of our neighbor girls. Let's be truthful about this, I was friends with more than one. This girl's dad had just bought a new farm tractor and had put in a portable sixty gallon farm gas tank. The man who bought that new tractor would come up to me at church and shake my hand and in his palm were gas stamps that could be redeemed at the local gas pumps. His daughter and I had a lot of fun times. I think she thought I was rich! Even my dad wondered how I was doing it. I never told anybody until now.

Robert Huston

About five miles from our farm was a little town called Mount Jackson. That is where all of us farm kids went to school. Mount Jackson High School had a baseball field behind it, where we all played ball. Did you ever hear of "car baseball?"

Let me explain this to you. You had one car at home plate, one car at the pitcher's mound, one in left field, one in center field, and one in right field. It was safest to play it at midnight. The fellow on the pitcher's mound would blink his lights indicating that he was ready. The second time he blinked his lights, he started for home plate. The fellow at home plate headed for first base. The car in center field would try to cut him off before he reached second base. If he did, he was out. Then the right fielder moved to home plate, and we started "car baseball" over again.

As you can see there were a lot of close calls. No one wanted to give up easily. One fellow had made it to second and then turned heading to third. To keep from being out he took off across the infield and hit the pitcher's mound with his front wheel, turning the car on its side. No one was hurt, but how were we going to set the car back up at that late hour? We didn't want to leave any evidence of our game.

One of our friends lived on a farm a mile out of Mount Jackson. Trouble came when we had to wake his dad and tell him what had happened. That was the only time it dawned on us that we shouldn't be playing "car baseball." His dad brought his tractor and a heavy rope and pulled the car back up on its wheels. Only the side mirror was broken. Car baseball came to an end that night with the outfield and the infield torn up for questions the next morning.

The next day the principal called a special school assembly. He wanted to know what "hare-brained guys" would stoop so low to tear up the high school ball field. Of course, no one knew anything. Not even the dad who helped put the car back upright. As Juniors and Seniors, in the spirit of community, we offered to fix up the field and to reseed it. It was the least we could do. Those 'hare-brained boys' were never caught.

OLD MAN SWIZZLE

Halloween has been around for a long time! People from all over the world have embraced it in a number of ways. Whether it is a good holiday or not is debatable! The name is not always the same! How people celebrate is not always the same. I have been with people who take this day to clean up family grave sites and stay there all day and night. They have brought lunch for the whole family. This was done out of love. In one case where ground was scarce the graves were walled crypts about five feet high in rows. A candle was placed on an open shelf at the beginning of the crypt, which they lit on this day.

In America, we look at the holiday far differently. We dress up and go to our neighbors' houses in the evening, and try to scare them. When they answer their door we are dressed up in scary costumes and say "trick or else!" In the hills of Pennsylvania in the 1940s this worldwide holiday was observed quite differently. This was a time when you made your own fun! Sometimes it did get out of control!

Robert Huston

Since I'm writing about certain people I am changing the name of the town and people, they now live in a little town called Dipswitch, PA. Now in Dipswitch and the surrounding area we had the finest folks. They would help each other out any day of the year, but on Halloween, "look out!" The town of Dipswitch had a country store, a feed mill and a barber shop. Oh, yes, and a crossroads. This crossroads is the center of this story.

What is it about this one day of the year, late at night, with a full moon? I get goose-pimples thinking about it.

At midnight, some guys and gals of all ages, that lived in Dipswitch, would gather at the cross roads. They would come and compare notes.

"Who has stuff sitting out that we can borrow?"

Then off they would go in different directions. One group knew of a buckboard and pulled it to the square. Another group found a buggy and set it up next to the buckboard. They had a hard time getting the buggy. The owner had tied his German Shepherd dog to the wheel, and he wasn't too eager to let the buggy go. So the kids gave him a piece of meat and brought him along.

By the end of the scavenging there was: a brass washing machine with a kick starting motor under it and its tubs, a load of corn shucks–wagon and all, three barrels of cured tobacco, a roll of barbed wire, a post hole digger and a few posts. Farmer Green has some heifers down by his pasture that he moved closer to the barn. I don't know how they got these heifers, but they ended up in the square.

The moon was still out, and the spirits were flying high, and the square was filling up. They dug postholes in the square's four corners and set the posts. Then stretched the wire around the posts and made a gate.

I wonder if these Dipswitch people worked this hard at home?

Standing back and admiring their work, they all agreed that it needed something more! Someone made the suggestion, "What about Old Man Swizzle's still?"

A group decided to go over to Old-Man Swizzle's place, making as little noise as possible. When they got there, he was sitting on his back porch with his shot-gun across his knees.

What to do? They would be seen by the moonlight. As they crept closer, it looked like he was asleep! Then they noticed that his jug of "corn squeezings" was lying on its side empty. Old Man Swizzle was dead drunk and passed out! Even his favorite dog was as drunk as a skunk!

Someone came up with a brilliant idea. Since that still would be too hard to take down, and they were running out of time, why not take Old Man Swizzle, his chair, gun, dog, and jug, and that's what they did. This was going to be the best prank they had ever pulled off. By the time they got back to the square they had a problem.

Where were they going to put Old Man Swizzle "among all that stuff?"

Since the buggy was sitting across the wagon, and it looked pretty stable. They set him in it, chair, gun, jug and the dog. He really looked like "King for the Day." It was now 5:30 in the morning. No one had any sleep so they all went home. Halloween was over.

THE NEXT DAY AFTER HALLOWEEN

By noon the next day, the whole community ended up at the square. They marveled at all the stuff in the square. Where did it all come from? Not everyone was happy! Especially that woman who owned the brass washing machine! She had washed clothes over a scrub board and had saved her egg money for years, sending away to the Sears and Roebuck Company for that new machine. It had been delivered the previous week and she had only used one time. She was mad, and she wanted someone's hide big time.

The fellow who had the wagon had left it out purposely so he was not displeased, but his neighbor, Farmer Green wasn't too happy. Someone in the crowd offered to help him drive his heifers back home. It was more than likely the kids who took them in the first place.

What about poor Mr. Swizzle? There he sat, looking rather stately. Everyone was laughing at his expense. All of a sudden he woke up with a start! He looked around at the crowd making fun at him. He became highly irritated, stood up and his shotgun went off in the air. He fell backwards out of the buggy. People tried to help him, but he didn't want anyone to touch him. He was steamed! When the gun went off, the dog barked, and the heifers stampeded through the gate. At least they were heading home!

Old-Man Swizzle had a bad attitude after that towards everyone. He didn't know who to blame. The teenagers gave him a wide berth. When they met or passed him on the street they tried to apologize. Sometimes it was accepted, but most of the time he would squint his eyes and just grunt at them. The men who bought his "corn-squeezings" had to pay one third more than usual. Pay back I think.

That was the last year that the square in Dipswitch was the center of attention. With a growing population and people admitting that these types of pranks had gotten out of hand, a town constable was elected to control these happenings. Also the area was growing in number. State police were making themselves known in the area.

BLOWING FENCES

Down on Grandpa's farm it had been one of those springs that resulted in a series of severe thunder and lightning storms. We had some large oak trees lining the lane that had been hit and split wide open. One large tree had fallen across the road blocking it completely. That meant that the farmers south of us had no way of getting into town for supplies. Grandpa opened up the barnyard gate and cut a place in the fence behind the barn. This created an access through the edge of the pasture and out the lower gate, so our southern neighbors could get out. The question was, what to do with all the trees hit by the lightning? Some of them could be cut up for firewood, and some of the others for boards.

This was going to be quite a job. Mr. Welder, who had a saw mill was hired to cut up the trees. Grandpa stored all the firewood he needed from the trees and Mr. Welder took the logs for his mill. As time progressed, there was more firewood than Grandpa needed, he sold the rest to anyone that was interested in buying it. After about three weeks all of the firewood was sold, Mr. Welder had taken everything useful for the mill, and all that was left were the large stumps sticking out of the ground. Mr. Welder said he could dynamite the stumps out. That was something that I wanted to see. I begged my mom and dad to let me go down to Grandpa Sam's when they were going to dynamite those stumps. At first, Mom was against me going. Dynamite was all she heard! I told her I would stay back. In time, I wore her down. I went back down to Grandpa's farm for the next two weeks.

Mr. Welder used an auger to drill many holes around the stumps. He would then shove a stick of dynamite into the hole, place a cap and fuse in it and then pack it in. He would then light the fuse and run about fifty yards away behind a tree. After the dynamite went off, the stump would loosen up a little bit but did not come out. So Mr. Welder would repeat until the stump came out. I thought there would be a big bang, but because it was deep in the ground there was just a "poof." Finally, all the stumps were out, all logs were loaded, all the firewood picked and the neighbors started using the road again.

Some of the dynamite caps and fuses were left over. Grandpa Sam put it high up on the shelf in the shed, so it would be safe and out of the hands of his grandson, me.

After awhile my friends, Bill and John, on the neighboring farms got bored. I remembered about the dynamite! It just seemed right to us that something ought to be done with that dynamite, it was just sitting up there on the shelf collecting dust. We knew that my grandparents, my parents and their parents would never allow us to handle that dynamite. So it had to be done in secret and at night. I got the dynamite, the fuses and caps. My friends brought the rifles for each of us. We ran around the hill, across from the farm, and hung the sticks of dynamite with the cap in them on the fence. Then from a safe distance we starting shooting those sticks of dynamite to make them explode.

How did we see late at night? It was the time of the full moon. When the moon came out from behind the clouds we would cut loose. We would hit those sticks and off they would go, causing a lot of excitement! Finally when all the sticks were blown up, it was early morning.

All the neighbors had heard the rifle fire and explosions, and so had Grandpa. He had gotten up early and discovered the dynamite missing! Needless to say, I wasn't allowed to be at Grandpa's farm for a long time. All my friends were grounded for a while! But that is not the end of the story!

We had broken the fence setting off the dynamite, and no one really noticed. Grandpa's young heifers and bull got out and ended up all over the township. Every week, Sam would get a call saying "Sam, some of your heifers came in with my cows this morning. Do you want me to bring them home or will you pick them up?"

Grandpa would trudge down to the neighbors to collect the heifers. Grandma usually went with him, giving her a chance to visit. Over time, all the heifers were back on the farm. The fence was fixed but the young bull wasn't accounted for. Where was he? Grandpa and Grandma were sitting on the porch one night when they heard a bellowing off in the distance.

Grandpa asked, "Do you suppose that bull is still down in the swamp? He'll be wilder than ever by now!"

The word went out to all the neighbors to keep an eye out for that bull.

Grandpa once again needed help, so I was once again allowed back into his fold. Occasionally, my friends would come on their horses, and we would go down to the swamp area, and look for that bull! All of us heard him at night, and we saw him a number of times, but we couldn't corner him. Man, was he wild!

Grandpa came up with a plan. He tied two heifers to a tree to entice that bull, then he would drive him into the field by the barn. Grandpa assumed that the bull would follow the cows into the barn. It should work.

The heifers were tied, but we never saw that bull! So we finally gave up on that plan. The bull had pulled a fast one on us, about nine months later both of those heifers had calves. One a little bull and one a heifer, and they both had the same markings of that bull. We never did get that bull out of the swamp, but we did have some fun at his expense.

We had some city cousins that would sometimes spend a weekend on the farm. They were really easy to spook. Not being used to all the sounds at night down on the farm, away off in the distance that bull would bellow and frighten my cousins. We told them ghost stories and stories of monsters such as "big foot" living in the swamps. Explaining in detail that the monsters would only come out after midnight.

Two days later we took the cousins for a buggy ride, late at night and they had no idea where we were going. By the time we got to the road that went through the middle of the swamp, we turned out the lantern. On both sides you could see dancing lights coming off the swamp water created by the methane gas that forms in all swamps, creating an eerie and ghostly sensation. Then we saw bright lights here and there called 'fox fire' created by the rotten deteriorating logs. It is beautiful when you know what it is, but not when it is pitch black and you are scared!

This was time to tell the story of the Ghost In the Swamp. Someone slowly turned the lantern up, at the same time we heard a sound in the grass around the trees. It was that bull, but the cousins didn't know it. He wouldn't come into the light, just as if it was scripted, he bellowed. I tapped the lines to the horse's backside, and they went full speed until we got back to Grandma's house. I have never seen kids so scared. One of them ran upstairs and crawled under the covers. The other two clung to Grandma and would not leave her side. I never told them anything different to this very day!

COAL PIT AND STEEL MILL

I shouldn't be here, but God is not through with me yet. I survived my first and second heart attacks and I survived the Air Force without a scratch.

When Jean and I got married, I was already running heavy equipment for coal companies. I had worked for many coal companies in our part of the country. It was eastern Ohio, western Pennsylvania, and then down in West Virginia. The first story takes place near Lisbon, Ohio, which is south of us.

I was running a front end loading shovel and had loaded trucks all day in zero weather. I was just loading coal, had just refueled the shovel and changed a brake band that had wore out. I was standing in the cab trying to get warmed up as you can understand in zero weather. You get pretty cold after an eight hour shift or ten hour shift. I just changed the band and I was standing in the cab and was trying to get warmed up just from the heat of the engine. I had just turned my head, and a large chunk of dirt started to come past my window in the cab. Now you must understand that you dig coal down in a pit about eighty foot deep and the cover dirt has been lifted off of it. Now this pit was about eighty feet down and one hundred feet wide, so it was a nice wide pit. I was setting sort of in the middle of that pit. I had just changed the band and . . . actually being in the middle of the pit is a very safe place to be. And it was below zero, so what could go wrong?

So the high wall actually on the other side of the pit was actually frozen, and in this kind of weather, you don't expect any sort of problems and really nothing should have happened. All of a sudden the frozen eighty foot high wall begun to crack and fall in. I saw a few chunks of dirt passing my cab, I couldn't even see the high wall. The drag line was sitting up on the hill was blowing his horn like crazy. I saw the chunks of dirt and him blowing his horn I knew that something was happening that was very unusual.

I heard a voice telling me to move back in the shovel out of the cab area. I moved between the engine and what was called the A-frame, which was the strongest part of the shovel. At that moment, the frozen high wall fell on the cab and completely smashed it. These large chunks of frozen dirt came down on all sides and even on the other side of the shovel. It sounded like a bomb going off.

"Only by the Grace of God, go I."

If I hadn't moved that day, I would have been killed immediately, crushed. Even if I had ran on the other side of the shovel and gotten off, I still would have had large chunks of frozen dirt of eighty foot high wall coming down on that shovel.

Grandpa Rocks!

Later on, I moved to the coal loading shovel up to the drag line, which was the machine that moved the dirt off the coal in the first place, and it sat up about one hundred feet above that pit. The drag line had two cables that control the bucket. One pulled the bucket in and out and the other cable picked up the bucket. It sounds very, very simple, but don't you believe it. You have to be very coordinated to run a drag line.

Both cables, when they are brand new, don't present any danger at all. It's when they become worn and have barbs on them, having been stretched beyond safety. That's when you would actually change it, before it breaks. No one actually knows when that cable has stretched as much as it's going to stretch, and when it's going to break. You just have to call it, and sometimes you change it before and sometimes you don't. It's best to change it before, I can tell you that.

Now, there is a problem when there is too much stretch, and it has stretched too much. When you wait too long, it's when it breaks and sometimes it comes back into the machine. Sometimes it goes down into the machine itself, sometimes it'd be just like a spring under load and then it all of a sudden snaps like a rubber band and sometimes it comes back into the cab where I sat. One could be cut up really, really bad and I have seen that happen to other operators, but that has never happened to me. You must understand that a cable only breaks when it's under a severe strain. When you are pulling it in through rock and dirt it sometimes breaks and comes back into the machine.

The cable that lifts the bucket only breaks at the top of the boom and sometimes comes down the boom like an angry spring. You never know where it's going to go. I never got hurt, and then because of the high cost of the cables, most companies want you to make it last as long, as long as possible. It makes sense, but it's still dangerous. I have seen that happen to where it comes down the boom, and just curls like a snake. It's much simpler to take the cable off before it goes that far. It's easy to change, as you can imagine with it all curled up you have to take a cutting torch and cut it up into small pieces so you can take one piece at a time. You have to be very, very careful that you don't hurt yourself, those barbs are just like knives.

I'm going to move from that situation to my first day on the job with a new coal company. Now, this is still going to be in the middle of winter before I knew how to run heavy equipment. This was before all this happened. This is the time that I didn't even have the boots to wear to work down in the pit, and I was using a hand shovel.

I was working down where they were loading coal and I was cleaning up in front of that loading shovel. So this goes a few years before I ever got on heavy equipment.

On the first day I arrived about 6:00 a. m., I didn't want to be late for my first day on the job. I was just getting out of my car when the owner came driving up at a very high rate of speed. He said, "Bob, don't go down there to that pit until I check it out because a neighboring coal company had their shovels and drag line blown up last night."

Grandpa Rocks!

What a way to come on a new job. He was right. As we walked down and we go closer we could see primer cord running all over the ground.

Primer cord is a type of explosive that connects to other explosives, and this is what we found. By that time, the state police had shown up, and all the rest of our people at the coal company. They had checked out the different pits and everything was all right, but the pit that I was going to work in, this is what we found.

The drag line had six large sticks of dynamite in around the engine underneath the A-frame. The boom would have dropped and blown up that machine. In the high lift, we found four sticks of dynamite down along the engine. In the drilling machine, we found two sticks of dynamite, and in the shovel, there were five sticks. When I say "sticks of dynamite," I don't mean something that's twelve inches long, I'm talking about sticks of dynamite that were about five inches around and probably five feet long. So, that's a lot of dynamite.

But why didn't it go off? The cap on the end of the primer cord was defective. Of course, when they lit it, the cap didn't go off. That's what saved all of our equipment.

My first day on the job working for Penn Coal instead of using that shovel I was talking about I became a guard. I carried a gun. If anyone that I didn't know came close, I fully intended to use it. I worked from 10:00 p.m. at night to 7:00 in the morning for two weeks. By this time, the West Virginia people had settled their strike, and everything was all right.

This has happened a couple times in our area where people have come out and tried to stop our coal companies in our area from mining or from actually stripping coal. This has happened over the years.

I am going to tell you an unusual happening. When I did work for the Penn Coal Company and I was an operator by this time, and it takes place in a coal pit outside Enon Valley, Pennsylvania.

You will notice that most of my stories are from Unity, Ohio, Enon Valley, and about a fifty mile radius. This is where I lived and where I worked. Enon Valley was the place where we went to church too, but this is also, where one of the coal pits is outside Enon Valley.

So it is now three days before Thanksgiving, we're in this coal pit, and we are digging off the dirt so we can get to the coal. Under this dirt, there is a layer of clay and this clay is what you make white bricks with. This is the only place in our state where you can get clay that makes white brick. White brick is very, very hard to make. Under the dirt was this clay.

To do this one has to take the dirt off to get to the coal, on one side we moved the dirt off, but we dug what is called a 'key way'. A key way is on the edge of the move. Since we had broken up the move with dynamite before, we thought all of it had gone off. We were wrong. As we dug into the key way, we found some primer cord that hadn't gone up yet. We didn't know how much more dynamite was there behind that left over from that explosion. We thought that most of it had actually been blown up. We thought that there was enough dirt on it that it wouldn't cause any problem. So, we relit that primer cord. We thought it was still safe. Well, we were very wrong.

Grandpa Rocks!

We relit it and it went off like a huge cannon. But what we didn't know was the concussion of the explosion went down to the valley right in line with the house. Now, that house was almost a mile away. The lady was getting ready for Thanksgiving the next day. The whole house started shaking and the cabinets opened up and all of the dishes fell out on the floor.

Pictures fell off the wall. And some of her plaster cracked. It wasn't very long that Penn Coal got a call from a very irate woman.

The owner of Penn Coal took the woman that day, the day before Thanksgiving, down to Beaver Falls, Pennsylvania, where there was a Meyer China Company. They made very good dishes. He bought her a complete of the very, very best set of china dishes that Meyer China made, and even put them in her cabinets for her. Needless to say, Penn Coal wasn't a popular for some time to come.

Another story that happened down in that very pit is this. I was loading coal and clay in that pit. While I was digging and loading coal, at the upper level, I came across a huge black rock embedded in the coal. It was a meteorite–very, very heavy, very, very hard, and very, very black. I was trying to get a truck to haul it home for me and that was the next day. I couldn't get anybody to do it. But the bulldozer man didn't know it, and he pushed it over the hill. And to this day, I'm very sad about it because it was in perfect shape. It was something that you could take to the Smithsonian Institute and it would be on display because it is very rare that you get a meteorite that hasn't exploded. This one didn't explode and it was about the size of, maybe, two bowling balls, something like that.

At the lower level, I was loading clay. In front of me was a clay face about fourteen feet high. All of a sudden a huge chunk of clay fell out and behind it was something that was prehistoric. Now, clay is nothing more than sea bottom. This clay was down over one hundred and twenty-five feet. So can you imagine, this was sea bottom at one time and eighty feet above it was slag, so this was a huge ocean at one time. So, here it was, fourteen feet high, eighty foot down and here was this something in there that was prehistoric. That's what I'm going to talk to you about.

There before my eyes was a huge cypress log outline in black, rotted coal. But the most exciting thing was that a large prehistoric fish was also outline by rotten coal. It was about five feet long. When I hit it with my teeth, it fell apart, and it was gone. But there it was; a fish and a cypress log had gone down in that slurry. Now, maybe this was the time of the flood, I don't know. They talked about slurries all over the world, and here it was, right in front of me.

Just lately in 1999, after a South Sea's storm, which was a very severe storm, a fish, just like the one that I had dug out was washed up on a beach on one of the South Sea islands. What we thought was prehistoric and not completely not alive anymore; well, there it was on the beach and it was the same type of fish that I saw in the face of that fourteen foot clay face. Now, I thought that was very interesting.

Grandpa Rocks!

I'm going to change from working in the coal fields. Some of the things were dangerous, but it was dangerous times. I am going to jump to the time that I no longer worked for the coal companies. I went to work for a steel mill service that serviced the steel mills in our area. Our job was to take hot slag out of the mill to a pit area which was about a quarter of a mile away. We wet it down, ran it over a separator and sold it back to the mill for their next heat, nothing was ever wasted. All types of metal go into a heat, and then there's always metal left over. Then the slag that came off of that was used for road beds. Everything was resold and recycled.

The company I worked for operated all over the world and had an established a system that was safe, quick, and it saved the mills lots and lots of money. But as the workers saw us cleaning up their pit of hot slag and steel, it all looked so easy. They began to put pressure on our company to let their people do the job. But they wanted to keep our safety men and our foremen over their men, which was very unusual.

I was a safety man and a foreman, along with twenty other mill service people. I will say this that when you get somebody who can get the job really well done, it always looks easy, but you don't realize how much skill it takes to do a good job. That's why it looked easy. But the job was anything but easy.

Well, we voted, all the foremen, not to do this because it was the most unsafe thing anyone could do. We knew how to do it; they thought they did–their men, and another thing, their men never ran heavy equipment before. They never or even knew how to roll out molten steel and keep it in small pieces that had to be done so we could load it onto our truck, which they were made special trucks. And they had to be small enough to get out the door. It looked easy. But it's not easy. It's just like rolling up taffy, and like taffy, there's weak spots in taffy. This is the way steel is. You find where the weak spot is, you tear it off and roll it up into a small piece. Now that's easy said, but it takes years to know how to do this.

We had outside men who had ran front-end loaders for years, and they were the best of the best of operators. They would not even consider working in a high heat and with molten steel. In that kind of atmosphere, our company let them roll over us and made us put their people on our equipment, and they didn't know how to even operate.

There are not enough adjectives to describe the way all of the foremen felt, and the danger our company put us in. I've never forgiven Small Mill Service for doing this to us.

Now here comes the problem. These people decided to give all the foremen as little cooperation as possible. We were outsiders, of course.Five times in these working conditions, I should have been killed.

"Only by the Grace of God, go I."

We had special trucks made to haul slag and steel, and they all had bathtub liners in them. These liners were about one inch thick steel. With high heat and time, they became warped, so there were small pockets that held water. It was very dangerous. When it rains, we left the truck beds up so that the water would run out of them. But once the bed was down, some of the water would run into these little warp spots. The workers from the mill, had to be told time and time again, when it rains, you don't put hot slag into a wet bed quickly. They were supposed to put it in very, very slowly. In other words, trickle it in so the heat from the slag would dry up the water. The worker mind set assumed they knew our job better then we did. So they just sometimes dropped the hot slag in one full swoop, blocking pockets of water. This would cause steam to form and cause an explosion so strong that the mill dust, four stories high, came raining down from the rafters. There's nothing more dangerous and more powerful than steam that is contained like that.

STEEL MILLS, UNIONS AND HEART ATTACKS

After six weeks of recuperating from my heart attack, the reclaiming service, and being home a lot, you would look at me and I looked fine, but inside I was really a basket case. The reclaiming service wanted me to see their doctor. Of course, he found me fit to work, but restricted me to only light work. I went, back to being a safety man and a foreman at the mill. I had also gone to my own heart doctor in Salem, and he had checked me out and he couldn't find anything. But my nerves were not completely healed.

In fact, while I was laid up the conditions in the mill working with some of their people had really reached a peak. All the foremen and safety men were having the same kind of problem. Everything that we did had to be timed with the pouring of steel in the pit. The loaders and the trucks had to be in and out of the pit on time. If you didn't take advantage of those and this timing, you didn't get your work done. It was unsafe, too. But if the driver decided to do it differently, and you were not where he needed you to be, you were in trouble. Or if he would linger out in the yard when he took a load of hot steel out and not come back right away, and you had a man in the pit waiting on him, you held one of his own men in the pit in that heat. You had to be in there with him, so there were two men standing waiting on that truck.

I had a loader setting in that pit in the heat waiting for a couple of trucks to come back. Knowing we were there, they finished this one load, and they decided they would stop to eat their lunch. Then they went to the bathroom leisurely–took a smoke–leisurely. I finally pulled the man out of the pit, realizing they weren't coming back, and they laughed about it. They, more or less, gave me the finger.

Well, that was it for me. I had just had it. I knew that they couldn't clean out the pit without me being there and if they were going to give me a hard time, I was going to give them a hard time back. I was not going to try any more to outsmart them, starting twenty minutes before I needed them, and when they didn't come back and they held me in that pit with that man, that was it for me.

I took my Thermos bottle and I went home. So the truck, high lift operators and everybody just sat there until the end of the shift, and then they went home. In other words, I shut down the job.

The next day, a meeting was called with all the parties involved, and anyone in an authoritative position. The Union, the steel and the service people were all there, and I was in the middle. My people started giving me a hard time, starting to blame me for everything that went on in that mill and for walking out.

Well, that was the wrong thing to do. My nerves inside weren't the best anyway. And, you know if a sleeping dog is asleep, you don't kick him. Well, they kicked me and kicked me hard, belittling me in front of all the authority in the mill and the Union. I stood up in the middle of those men and told them that they had made the dumbest agreement with the Union and with the mill. As far as that Union was concerned, it was the worst Union I had ever seen. We had been in mills all over the world, and that Union was completely out of control. They were robbing the mill every day with some of the things the Union men would let them get away with and created the most unsafe environment I had ever seen.

I told them that labor relations should be brought into that mill, and they should shut it down until they get it right. I said that my company thought more of the almighty dollar than they did for the safety of their own men and equipment. Well, I thought I was going to be fired on the spot, so I let it all out. It really felt good.

Now the Union that day was very quiet, and the steel people admitted that they had a real problem working in the mill with the Union. But it had been like that for years, but there was really no answer to the problem. The mill service people's faces were white. As white as I have ever seen. I don't know if they were ready to kill me, but I know they were very, very mad, and I think they thought they were going to lose their contract. I think maybe it was just a little bit of both.

Robert Huston

On the back of my safety jacket, I had painted, "Christian." Now, of course you wore a safety jacket, a safety vest, safety hat, safety shoes, safety gloves because you were working around heat. That was my uniform. Two days later, secretly, the Superintendent of the steel company, came to me and said, "Bob, I've been waiting to say what you said the other day for years. Thank you, thank you, my friend for standing up for what is right."

Of course, now, the whole mill knew that a mill service foreman had blown his top. They had been watching me work with their people in the mill area and they said this, "If Huston can't get it done and blows his top, then something must really be wrong."

They admitted my Christian way with handling their people on the job was extraordinary. There was something else in that mill with their people. They had many blacks that worked for them, that's the steel people did, and some of those men had come to me quietly and shook my hand and said, "Now I know this is what being a Christian really means. I'm glad to know you." Now, that made me feel huge.

Of course, the mill service people weren't too happy with me and they let me alone for a long time and I didn't get fired. But here is what they did do. At the end of each year they would evaluate your job, you and how you handled it. There's about thirty questions on it, and then you would sign it. Then you would get a five or eight percent raise. When I got my evaluation, there's an A, B, and C on every question—on the thirty questions. There was A and B on all of them. Somebody had erased and gave me a C and D the whole way through. When I saw that, that made me so mad that I said, no way am I going to sign that, and threw it down on our superintendent's desk, and said, "Who had the gall to erase all that?"

Nobody said anything. I don't know whether that year I got a raise or not. It may have been automatic. I don't remember.

At Christmas time, our mill was shutting down for eight days. This is very, very rare, but they were shutting down for Christmas for some kind of repairs that had to be done, and the mill couldn't be running. So, all the men, then, had Christmas off. All of us. I was thrilled with that, the idea of being home all that time for Christmas. Well, we also had a job at another steel mill, and what they did they let some of those men off and took our men and moved them into their slots over Christmas and told us we had no choice. It was either that or quit. Guess who was on that list? Good old Bob Huston.

They would not deviate from that. So, when our mill was shut down for those eight days, I still had to work all eight days at the other steel mill. I couldn't afford to get laid off.

Now, this has never been done before. The mill service that I worked for was trying to get a contract with US Steel. A truck and machine were assigned to me and another foreman. We were told not to refuse any job. Also, we took that same machine underneath the mill, but way, way back and dug out some different things. What I didn't know the machine they give us had a bad starter. They knew it had a bad starter when they give it to us. Now, that machine could have stopped anywhere while we were doing these things way back in the mill. I don't know how we could have ever got it out if it couldn't come out of its own power. Now, they knew that starter was bad. They also knew that I was going to be the operator that was going to be running it. By the Grace of God, that starter never gave me one minute's trouble the whole time we was up there until the day we were to load it onto a lowboy trailer. And the starter wouldn't work. It just so happens that I made friends with some of the people in US Steel in Pittsburgh.

They had a crane operator that was in there doing some work. They lifted up the machine and put it on the lowboy trailer for me. They were actually, they were sticking it to me is what they were doing. I brought this machine back to Midland, and I had a pickup truck that they assigned to me. I took the pickup back to where I had got it that same day, and they didn't know where the pickup was or where I was. They said that I had stole it. Well, I had already signed off on the pickup and went back to my job in Youngstown. They were trying as much as they could to get me in trouble. Now that's three things they did to me.

Another thing happened in the steel mill. Years ago there was a problem, the blacks did not get promoted in this steel mill in Youngstown. The Union did one good thing. They said since these men hadn't got promoted, they should get a financial restitution, they should get some kind of money. So they worked it out with the steel mill in Youngstown and give each black man two thousand dollars. They had so much money left over that they gave two hundred dollars to all the young blacks that were working there that weren't even born yet when the other men hadn't had any advancement in the mill. They just overlooked them. So that's some of the things that go on in the mill.

After all the things that I am telling you, in October of that year, I had my second heart attack. I had gone back to work too soon. It was six months to the day when I had my first heart attack at Blackwater Falls, West Virginia. I called my doctor in Salem again, and we set up a time when he was going to check me out one more time.

They strapped me to the table and did a catheterization, and couldn't find anything. What was causing me to have these heart attacks? They looked me over and back, and then did it again. I went into shock. They packed me in ice and once again they flipped me and they found my heart turned over in its socket, and that the back of my heart about three inches long, it was blocked. There was no way that could be fixed.

Well, I'm going to say something about God in His graciousness and His design of the human body. You know you can lose half of your body and still function. You have two legs, two arms, two eyes, two ears, two kidneys, two lungs, but you only have one heart. Around that heart, you have a double set of muscles or arteries that can be used. Since those were blocked in the back of my heart, the two sets of muscles came into play. All I had to do was eat right, exercise and don't do strenuous work, and these muscles would gradually take over. That's what I needed. So the other set of blood vessels have been working all this time. It has been since 1981 that this all took place, and I am now seventy-nine. Of course, it wasn't very long after that, I quit working in the steel mill.

BRUSH PILE, FLYING SAUCERS

On Sunday mornings before church, I would go out onto the back porch and talk to God and review my notes for my Sunday school lesson. This Sunday the Holy Spirit led me to go out onto the back porch to look for honey. For this Sunday's lesson, I needed honey, four fish, and some loaves of bread. So I was in the Spirit and I walked back out into our yard, around a grove of Locust trees, around the brush pile and didn't see anything and sat back down on the porch. I needed this honey for an illustration. And the Lord said, "Go out and look in your yard."

So, again I got off the porch and walked around the property and as I came back past the brush pile, I looked down at this log. There was about four pounds of honey hanging on this log. I gently pulled this log out of the brush pile.

Now, for four pounds of honey, it takes a lot of bees to be able to actually make this much honey. There was a few dead bees on it, so I got out one of Jean's meat plates, took one of her knives, and cut that four pounds of honey off of that log and brought it into the house. The lesson that day was, God Provides, in the past and He'll even provide today.

I took that honey to church, I cut it up and served it by the aisle of the church. Everybody had a piece of fresh honey that morning. Now, God knew what lesson I would have been teaching a year before I taught it, and He provided the illustration. Now, why didn't we see those bees? I don't know. But He did all of this in a year in advance before I needed it. If God can do that, why don't we trust Him?

It was another Sunday morning. I was out on my back porch again looking over my lesson. It was very early in the morning and again I was told to go out on the back porch, and I did. I heard policeman's sirens way off in the distance coming my way, which isn't unusual because there's always trucks or something getting into wrecks on Route 14. Today there were six to eight cars from different departments, State Police, the local Salem Police, and they didn't seem to be chasing anybody. As I looked out of my back porch up, they were looking at something shining in the sky. Later I found out that the Salem Police had found some shiny objects in the sky. They were flying erratically very fast back and forth. Pittsburgh Air Patrol reported that they had nothing on their scopes, so they begin to follow these objects east towards Ohio, passing my home along the way. When the Salem Police left, they called ahead and picked up the State Police and other law enforcement agencies that were out on the road that morning. Someplace over at Beaver Falls, the objects just disappeared.

That's just on this side of the Pittsburgh airport. They never scrambled because there was nothing on their scopes. They were, the police were looking at something in the sky. I heard the Salem Police were reprimanded for leaving their area. I think if I'd have been on patrol, I have done the same thing.

My lesson for that Sunday was, "Things in life that are not always as they seem." God had come through again with an illustration just when I needed it.

HYPNOTIST

I was in high school at Mount Jackson, Pennsylvania. A bunch of my friends went to New Castle to the Casilton Cathedral. This was an unusual night; a famous hypnotist was putting on a show. We were all awestricken at what he was able to do.

First, he took a one dollar bill from ten people, asking them each to write down the serial number on the bill on a piece of paper and place the paper in their pockets. Then he put those dollar bills into an envelope and put it in a folder on a table on the stage.

He took a number of people up on stage and proceeded to hypnotize them. This hypnosis took them back to their childhood. As he brought them back to the childhood, he was very careful what he allowed them to say!

Some of the participants talked 'baby talk', others threw tantrums. It was funny but we took it very seriously. His next instruction was for two fellows to put their arms straight out, locking them in place at his suggestion. Asking two younger children to come up on stage and hang on their arms to try to pull their arms down or apart. The kids even hung in mid-air on their arms but could not get them to come down. He brought these two men out of their hypnotic state and asked the young children to repeat what they had just done! This time they were able to pull down the arms easily. The hypnotist snapped his fingers and the two fellows slipped into a deep sleep again.

Now he asked the people with the serial numbers of the bills to take them out and look at the numbers. They were to clear their minds of all else. He opened that folder and took out one envelope at a time, still sealed. He then hollered out one serial number after another. The people that held the serial numbers verified that he was correct in what he read.

After this he cleared the stage, he asked people who had a drinking problem, those who smoked too much, and those who gambled too much, to come up on stage if they wanted help. He wanted people who really wanted to quit these habits. To our surprise, about twenty men and women came up on stage.

"If you admit this in front of strangers, you can be helped," he instructed.

Calling for extra chairs, he put the smokers in one section, the drinking people in another section, and the gamblers in a third section. Touching each one on the forehead, they fell into a deep sleep. As he walked by each person, he told them that the taste and smell of their addiction would be so pungent that they wouldn't be able to stand it anymore. The whole stage was filled with sleeping people.

Grandpa Rocks!

Then he asked some of his recovered patients, who were in the audience, to come up on stage. One by one they gave their testimony of how long they had their particular habit, and how long they had been recovered from it. He then had each one stand beside the chair of one of the sleeping people, touching the head of the sleepers, they woke up. As they woke up they started talking to the person standing beside them, the recovered person would then tell them their story and would give them encouragement. Wow!

What about the gamblers? The hypnotist gave them suggestions and planted them in deep in their mind, therefore blocking the adverse desires in their minds. Explaining to them that of all the addictions, gambling was the hardest one to control. After talking to everyone, the new recoveries were encouraged to keep in contact with the recovered people. Then he cleared the stage once again.

Then he asked the whole audience to concentrate on the eagle mascot that was on top of the stage ruffle. We all did laughingly and were told to listen to his voice.

"Empty out your mind and when I say stand up, stand up." A number of people in the audience and of the number of kids in my group stood up, including me!

"Come to the front." I did.

"Go up on the stage." I did.

"Sit in that chair." I did, falling immediately into a deep sleep. It was a peaceful deep sleep! Again the whole stage was filled with sleeping people! The rest of this I don't remember, but one of my friends took notes!

I sat there in a deep sleep. When the hypnotist said "Stand up," I did with my eyes wide open. Giving each of us a lemon, he told us it was the sweetest orange we had ever eaten. I guess the whole crowd went wild with all that slurping. Then he slid us back to sleep. He picked some participants to take a shower. As participants started to take off their clothes, the hypnotist ran around telling them to put their clothes back on. The crowd loved it! Then he said, "Everybody, back to sleep!"

I was one of the deepest sleepers. He had me stand up and hold out my hand. He explained to me that he was going to light a match and hold it under my hand, letting the fire go up between my fingers. He then stated that I wouldn't feel the heat and that it would not burn! I stood there with my hand out, unconcerned. The fire went up between my fingers and I did not have one burn! Wow!

He now gave us all a newspaper, and told us the war was over. When he snapped his fingers we were all to go into the audience and try to sell the newspaper. That's what we all did. We gradually came out of that sleep and realized what fools we were making out of ourselves.

The next day at the school assembly my friends and I told this story. This happened just as I wrote it, but I don't remember half of it.

BEN AND TESSIE

There were two slaves that grew up on a plantation in Georgetown, the girl's name was Tessie and the man's name was Ben. Tessie's mother and father died, leaving her an orphan. They had been slaves on the plantation for years. Tessie was born on the plantation and worked with her parents. She was so young when they died that they took Tessie into the main house. The Hendersons are the owners of the plantation in Georgetown. They had a young girl named Elizabeth. Little Elizabeth was the apple of her father's eye, and anything she wanted, she got. Elizabeth and Tessie spend as much time together as possible. Now, after two years Elizabeth asked that Tessie be her own personal slave. Her father said yes, but she would have to keep Tessie in her rightful place. In Tessie's life, after losing her parents and having this friend of Elizabeth, it became the happiest days of Tessie's life.

Elizabeth and Tessie became inseparable friends. Everything that Liz learned, especially etiquette, she taught to Tessie. Everything Liz was taught in school, she also taught Tessie. It was the happiest time of Tessie's life. Their joy was only marred by the fact that no one could know what Liz taught Tessie, Tessie had to stay in her place.

There was a slave known as Ben. He was six years older than Tessie and was in charge of all of the blacks on Henderson Plantation. He was a good man, but he had to be hard on the other blacks, and it broke his heart. His position of responsibility brought him to the main house quite a lot, and he and Tessie became friends, and slowly but surely, they fell in love. Now, that's not allowed.

When Ben would take the slaves to the rice fields and drop them off, he always took the long way back, Tessie and Liz would meet him and teach him everything they had learned and everything they could. Nothing was ever written down, it was all done by memory. They had to be very, very careful. Ben and Tessie were like sponges, they wanted to know more, and more, and more.

They wanted to go north to Canada, but how would they ever do that and live? Three years passed, and Elizabeth got married, and moved away. Tessie was very lonely and cried for a week. Ben began to pray for a miracle. Nothing Ben could go could do would mend Tessie's broken heart.

Something happened within the next year that is very rare where slaves are concerned. The Steven Plantation in West Virginia had lost their housekeeper. She had had a bad heart attack and died. Also, their main black foreman had an accident, and he had died. The Stevens and Hendersons were good friends, and the Stevens had visited the Hendersons and were impressed with Tessie and Ben. Recognizing that Tessie was very polished, very graceful, and Ben was very, very loyal. The Stevens inquired if the Hendersons would sell Tessie and Ben to them. The Stevens would send an overseer to escort them up north and bring the money with him. It took the Hendersons three months to make a decision, then they called Tessie and Ben in to break the news.

Tessie cried for a week, and Ben could do nothing to console her. The overseer arrived, and they took an instant dislike to him. He smelled of booze. There were many taverns along the way, and each night they stopped, the overseer would shackle them in the basement or in the horse stables, even in the rain.

Somewhere north of Pikesville, Kentucky, they had to ford a river. A well-dressed northern gentleman noticed Tessie and Ben and the overseer. This man made friends with the overseer. When the overseer wasn't looking, this gentleman looked right at Tessie and Ben, smiled and winked at them. Ben's heart jumped. He knew he could trust this man, but he said nothing to Tessie.

It was three in the afternoon, and the gentleman offered the overseer a ride in his buggy. He took him and the slaves to a little town twelve miles north of Pikesville, which had one of the best taverns in the country. This was music to the overseer's ears.

Ben and Tessie were tied to the post in the stable. The drinking started in earnest in the tavern. About nine o'clock, the northern gentleman brought food and water to the slaves. He said, "I will see you both at midnight. Be ready to travel fast."

The overseer came out around midnight too. Actually, he was going to check on the slaves and was so drunk, he passed out on the ground in front of Tessie and Ben. The northern gentleman arrived and removed the keys, bill of sales and the money the overseer had left. Putting the shackles on the overseer's legs, he tied him up, gagged him and put him further back in the stable among the corn shucks. The overseer would not be found for two or three days. Praise the Lord.

Tessie's prayers are answered, but there is a long way to go. Their next stop was the Ohio River, where they made contact with a man who had six barges of logs going up the river to Pittsburgh, Pennsylvania. There was a secret room near the main cabin, and Tessie and Ben slept sound for the first time in many, many days.

They came to a place called Three Mile Island, just south of Beaver, Pennsylvania, and they walked across the island and waited on the north side to be picked up. They were not allowed to build any fires, and sat down to wait as instructed. They almost froze to death. After four days, their food and water ran out and on the fifth day, a bunch of fishermen appeared with lanterns on their boats.

One of these boats came to shore and started to cook fish. Ben was going to have to trust his fellow man once again. So he came out of hiding and asked for some fish. The man said, "Stay out of the light! Stay out of the light! I will bring you something to you. We would have come sooner, but a lot of men from the Stevens Plantation are looking for you."

When night fell, he took the two slaves to a town along the Ohio River called Freedom.

Now, there was a religious colony that lived in Freedom known as the Shakers. They believe that Christ was coming back in their lifetime, so they never married. Ben and Tess had never seen so much love. It was hard to believe that there were people like this. Freedom was well-named. They stayed until early December. The Shakers gave them warm clothes, a map, and food, and sent them on their way north.

Traveling at night to avoid the people looking for them during the day, they came through a place called New Brighton, Pennsylvania, traveled up through Beaver Falls, and finally arrived in Darlington, Pennsylvania.

That evening an early snow blew in. They had been instructed to take the back road out of Darlington. Looking for their next landmark for a big tree that looked liked a spider sitting upside down, the snow began falling in earnest and the temperature was dropping rapidly. After many hours they found the tree. The next landmark was a big red brick house with four chimneys, on the top of a hill.

The snow was still coming down, when finally they saw a house high on a hill. Ben says, "Honey, don't give up. Just a step at a time. They walked one step at a time, and they were getting closer, but cold fatigue was taking its toll. Ben was half carrying Tessie by the time they got to the Luke house. Now, they could see the Lukes sitting down for supper, then Ben collapsed Tessie made it one half way to the door, then she collapsed. They had almost made it, and they knew they were going to freeze to death a few steps from freedom.

Now, the Lukes had just had their blessing and were starting to pass their food when a knock came to the front door. They all heard it. Mrs. Luke said, "Who would be out in this kind of weather? Goodness, mercy!"

She took the oil lamp and opened the front door and looked outside. Seeing nothing she closed the door and went back to the table and started passing the food again.

Another knock, louder this time was heard at the front door. The whole family, all of them, grabbed their oil lamps and came out on the front porch. The wind started blowing harder, and they suddenly saw a red scarf blowing in the snow out in the yard. They all ran out and picked up Tessie. She opened her eyes and pointed to the road, saying, "Ben, Ben," and then she collapsed. Luke and the boys found Ben, but he didn't move.

Getting Ben and Tessie into the house, the Lukes worked as a team. They took off their frozen clothes, wrapped Ben and Tessie in blankets and set them in front of the fireplace. Then they started putting warm soup, one teaspoon at a time, into their mouths. Finally, their eyes opened. Tessie started to cry, letting it all out. The Lukes cried, too, and they all thanked God.

The question that is still asked today is "Who knocked on the door, twice?

Tessie and Ben stayed with the Lukes all winter, and in the spring they made it to Canada.

Now, Mr. Luke told me this story years ago. The Luke's were part of the Underground Railroad, a station along the way. Maybe it was their two guardian angels that knocked.

LIFE STORY AND DREAMS

My life has been interesting, interesting enough to share with you. I realize that God is in complete control of my life, even when I didn't know it. Some of these things that have happened to me over the years have been very unusual. When I was in Germany, I realized that dreaming was very important. There were many times I went away for the weekend on sightseeing tours. This was one of those weekends.

A friend and I went into a little town, I don't even remember the name. It was evening when we arrived and we got a room in one of the hotels. This little town was unique, set in among the mountains. All of the hotels there seemed to have balconies. Our room overlooked the valley and mountain area. This is where the first part of this dream took place.

It was early in the morning, I had just gotten up and was looking over the valley from the balcony. It was a pretty little valley, as the town flowed down among the mountains. I noticed two mountain peaks; one to the left and one to the right with the sun was coming up between these two mountains. It was a beautiful sunrise. At the base of the mountains, among the pines, was a little church. It wasn't a large church about the size of a little community church. People were starting the walk to early morning services. The bell was tolling in the distance, and you could see the people one by one with their heads bowed, their coats up around their necks going into the church, two by two, some holding hands, some not. I don't even remember getting out of bed. I just remember standing there taking this all in. The mist in the valley was beginning to rise and the sound of the bell ringing in the distance was more than I could absorb.

Why the Lord brought me here to show me this little site I still am not fully aware of today, but I know that it had a deep effect on me. I must have been standing there for a while. Eventually, I felt somebody tugging at my shoulder and shaking me. It was my buddy.

He said, "Bob, what's wrong with you? What's going on? I've been shaking you for fifteen minutes. Are you sleeping? Are you in a dream?"

"Really, I don't know. I don't know what's going on," I replied.

After being discharged, I came home. The Lord woke me up one night and showed me. As I was sitting up in bed, I had just dreamt this dream again with every detail so very, very vivid. There was nothing that my mind had left out. This time as I was standing there, viewing this scene, I felt that presence of the Almighty God in my dream.

I didn't dare look around to see who was standing next to me. Instead of my buddy's hand being on my shoulder shaking me, I felt the hand of Almighty God upon my shoulder. I felt the Presence of the Lord standing beside me. I knew that he was dressed in white light? As I thought about this dream and felt the Presence of the Lord, I wanted it to end because I was getting scared, and yet I wanted it to last because I didn't want to have His Presence to leave me. It was an awesome, awesome thing.

In high school, I dreamt I was somewhere in the Himalayas. I was staying in a little shack at the foot of the mountains. Even today I can recall the shack in vivid detail. Now, I've never been in the Himalayas, but this shack is very, very real.

I got up. It was early in the morning. There was a path that sort of wound up over the valley and up into the mountains, I was walking up this path. Walking into the mists of the valley and through the rocks, I went higher and higher. As I walked up this path, I walked around a rock at the edge of the mountain.

Lo and behold! There was a hole in the rock. You couldn't see it, only if you hadn't stumbled upon it. I walked through this hole in the rock; there was a set of stone steps that went up into the interior of that mountain. I climbed slowly because I was scared. I didn't know why I was there, and began to realize that what the old man who occupied in the shack at the foot of the mountain had told me the day before. I'd come to him and I said to him, "I would like to have wisdom. I would like to have and find peace within my life. And I would like to have an assurance of where I could find this and where to go."

"Don't worry. A way will be opened unto you and find peace in your life," he replied.

Robert Huston

All of these things were running through my mind as I was going up these stone stairs: "A way will be opened unto you." I figured the old man must have known what he was talking about, but I realized that this old man did not live in that shack or on that mountain. Where he came from and where he went in my dream, I have no idea, but I knew that he was there to help guide me on my way to peace and the answer to some of my questions that I was looking for.

There I was, going up the secret stairs and walking gradually to the top of the mountain. It seemed like I climbed for hours, then I felt the anticipation and the Presence of the Lord growing, and I was just getting goose pimples all over. Finally, I walked up ahead and I saw two huge rocks. Being drawn, I walked between these two huge rocks. Just as I just got through them, for some unknown reason I could not go any further. My feet would not move, my body would not move. As I stood there I saw this beautiful sunset coming up again up over the edge of the mountain. As the sun came up, I saw a walled city. All I could see of it was the corner of the city and just the very edge of the gate. Try as much as I could, I could not see anymore. I tried to move to get closer because I was being drawn toward it, but I could not move. I knew without a question that I was in the Presence, in the Glory of God. I felt that this walled city was the corner of the City of God. As you can see, God was guiding me, even in my teenage years.

If you had known me in my teenage years, even though I looked like a Christian and walked like a Christian, went to church, and was a member of the Young People's Society, in no way was I a Christian. I didn't know the Lord, Jesus Christ. I had never given him my body and my soul. I did a lot of things that teenagers do, probably even worse than they do today. I was a counterfeit. God showed me. He taught me of His Presence, even though I had not asked Him into my life at that time.

There was quite a span of years between my teen years and the years I was in the service when God showed me His Presence, even through I was not a born again Christian. Now, wouldn't you know that God has for everybody who is in the sound of my voice and reading this book, that God does have a plan for your life. He has a real plan for your life. He brings all kinds of happenings to your life.

When I was stationed in Germany, I felt His Presence in this little town, God showed me the two rocks that were in my dream. Now, lo and behold, the two rocks that were in my dream even though I had never seen them before are in Burgessgarten, Germany, on top of one of those mountains.

Now, when I was there . . . maybe I should tell you what the Eagle's Nest is. This is where Hitler had built his home, and when I was there he had been bombed out, and he has a big picture window that looks down on the Alps, and he could see the Alps, the mountain ranges, in three countries. It's a very, very pretty sight. It's one of those awesome sights that you see that just takes your breath away. Even though this man was an agnostic, he did enjoy the beauty around him, even though he didn't understand it completely and why it was there. He didn't understand his place in life.

God took me up to the Eagle's Nest, and there you drive up the side of the mountain through a series of gates. Also at the bottom of the mountain was a set of buildings where the SS troops, the elite troops, guarded the mountain and Hitler when he was there. Up further at the base of this mountain, at the base of the very top of this mountain there's two huge gates. You walk back a long, long tunnel and you come into an elevator that goes to the top of the mountain. There at the top is what they call the Eagle's Nest.

I thought when I was there that they would restore that and keep it as one of the tourist sites, but they tell me now today that they have torn that building completely down. They don't want to have the people to have anything of Hitler to remember, because it was really a thorn in Germany's side. And they've torn it completely down. But the mountaintop is still there; the mountains are still there. And the Son that glorified the whole area is still there.

When you reach the top of the mountain, lo and behold, you walk up this path and you go off to the right and you walk between two huge stones. There is a little wood bridge with a railing. As you look down, you just look down for miles and miles and your eyes play tricks on you. When I was there and walked in between these two rocks, I had the oddest and the strangest feeling that I can imagine. Even though I didn't know why. And then when I came home and had these dreams again out of the service, the dream came back that I had in my teenage years.

This dream was reenacted again as a soldier, and I realized that these were the two rocks that I had in my dream back when I was a teenager. But this time I dreamt back in my room in Enon Valley, Pennsylvania. In the Lord's Presence, where before I couldn't get around the rock, and I couldn't move, He let me come around the wall and the rock. I started to walk towards the city. This time I not only saw the wall, but I saw the gates. The gates were open. It was as much to say, "The gates are open, you can come in, but you can only go so far."

Since that time, I have come to know the Lord, Jesus Christ as my personal Savior. I'm not a perfect person, but I did give my life, my heart, my mind and my soul to the Lord, Jesus Christ. I asked him to come into my life and control me, to guide and direct me. I really feel now that I will have one more dream, and that dream will probably be the day that I pass on out of this world.

God has worked in my life, I know that He is real. I don't doubt His Existence, I don't doubt what He can do. I fully understand what it means when He said, "Let Us make man in Our Image."

The Image of God dwells in me. I have intelligence and creativity. I have the ability of dominion. I know how to live in a community and share Christ. I understand the social part of being a Christian. So, when I die, I fully expect to see these dreams again. The one I had in the service, the one I had as a teenager. I expect to walk between these two rocks and walk up to the city gates. I am going to meet the Guardian Angel that has been watching over me for all my years. I am going to meet the other angels who greet me.

You say, how do you know this? Well, it's in scriptures that there will be angels at the gate to welcome you in. And inside the gate, I will see Christians, Christians who have given their life, their mind, their body and soul to our Lord, Jesus Christ. I'm going to see people I am related to and people that I have never met before. I'm going to see Paul and Enoch who walked with the Lord. I'm going to see Jesus Christ for the first time as He really is and I'm going to see God and the Holy Spirit.

These are things that I know, because of these dreams, that God has given these dreams to draw me to Him. To make me realize that He is real. And I just thank the Lord.

Printed in the United States
57668LVS00001B/160-261